The Big Festival of Lights

Stories and Plays for Hanukkah

MINT EDITIONS

The Big Festival of Lights: Stories and Plays for Hanukkah
contains work first published between 1903–1924.

ISBN 9781513201184 | E-ISBN 9781513127828

Mint Editions

**MINT
EDITIONS**
minteditionbooks.com

Publishing Director: Jennifer Newens
Design & Production: Rachel Lopez Metzger
Project Manager: Micaela Clark
Typesetting: Mind the Margins, LLC

Contents

David of Modin:
A Hanukkah Play

CAST OF CHARACTERS

DEBORAH, a widow of Modin
DAVID, her son
MIRIAM, her daughter
ABRAHAM, a servant in the household of Deborah
MATTATHIAS, the Asmonean
JUDAS ⎫
JOHN ⎪
ELEAZAR ⎬ his sons
SIMEON ⎪
JONATHAN ⎭
APOLLONIUS, commander of Syrian host
ALNASHAR, aide to Apollonius
AZARIAS, a Jewish traitor
SOLDIERS, SLAVES, ETC.

PROLOGUE

SCENE—*Dwelling of Deborah. Miriam on couch to the right. Deborah seated at table on the left. Before her are soldiers' garments, helmet, shield, and sword. Striking on shield heard three times without. Miriam starts up suddenly.*

MIRIAM: O David! Mother! What was that?

DEBORAH: My child, thou hast been dreaming. That was nothing but the sentinel striking thrice on his shield to signify that all is well.

MIRIAM: But David—where has he gone? 'Twas but a moment ago that I saw him face to face, as plainly as I see thee now.

DEBORAH: David? My child, what makes thee think of David now? 'Twas two years ago, when last I saw my only son, and he has not been here since. Ah! God only knows whether I shall ever behold his face again. Dost remember, Miriam, how thy brother asked me leave to go to Jerusalem, and how he started with his harp, one early morning, to gladden the holy city with his song? How all the people were sad, because David of Modin had left them to go to Jerusalem. Let us hope he is there in safety now. Let us pray that he has not fallen before the enemies of the Lord, who have defiled the holy city. Who knows? Perhaps he is now with the God of his fathers.

MIRIAM: Then it is all a dream.

DEBORAH: How strange, my child, that thou too, shouldst have been thinking of him now! But a moment ago I sent for the sword and shield of thy father. His helmet and robes are there too, and I was just thinking how my David would look, fighting for his God and his country. O David, where art thou? But tell me, dearest Miriam, how did he appear to thee? Art thou sure it was thy brother? Tell me, was his face joyful or sad?

MIRIAM: O mother, it was none other than he. I am sure, for I saw him thrice. At first he appeared to me, carrying his harp on his back. I noticed that its strings were rent asunder, and that his face was sad.

He seemed to regard me with a pitiful smile, and I advanced to take his hand, to speak to him words of solace, when lo! he suddenly changed, and I no longer beheld my brother, the minstrel, before me. In his place stood one with smiling face. On his head stood out the long ears of a jester. No harp could I see, but still it was David, for looking again, I saw the scar which he had received in his youth. The smile that played around his lips was not in his eyes, for gazing into them I seemed to look into his very soul, which was sad. Again he suddenly changed. This time I could see him better than ever. It seemed that he had never appeared so plainly to me before. He stood on an eminence, with sword in hand, and once more his harp was with him. He beckoned me to go to him. I did so, but, alas! as I stretched forth my arm, he suddenly vanished. The sound of battle rang in my ears, and—I awoke.

DEBORAH: Surely, my child, there is some meaning behind it all. Perhaps we have not hoped in vain. Someday, by the will of God, we may see him again, and if so, may it be as in thy last vision—with sword in hand. O, had the Lord but blessed me with *ten* sons! How happy I should be to send them to battle against the enemies of Israel! Happiest of women is the mother of the Maccabees, who so nobly defended our country and our religion.

MIRIAM: Yes mother, the camp of Mattathias is in need of such men as our David, and—*(Enter Abraham, bowing.)* Abraham! What is it? Is there any one without?

ABRAHAM: Ay. There are three men without, two of them sentinels, having in their charge a spy, a man who has just come down from Jerusalem, and is suspected of being an enemy to our cause. He asserts that he is a native of Modin. At least, so they tell me, and they have brought him here to see whether he speaks the truth. As I am newly in thy service, I do not know him, for he claims to be thy absent son David.

DEBORAH AND MIRIAM: David!

DEBORAH: Tell me, Abraham, does he bear a scar on his forehead?

ABRAHAM: Ay, near the left temple.

DEBORAH: Then it is he. Bring him to me at once. O Miriam, thy dream has come true!

(Enter David between two sentinels, who fall back as he rushes into his mother's arms.)

DAVID: Mother! Miriam! *(Takes his sister's hand.)*

DEBORAH: My son, I feared thou wert no more, and now I see thee before me. O merciful God! He, who left me when but a stripling, has returned in the full strength of years. How powerfully thou art built, my beloved! What brawny arms!

DAVID: Yes, mother, the Lord has been kind to me. He has saved me from the fate that befell so many in Jerusalem, and has blessed me with a strong arm to avenge those poor unfortunates. It is better fitted now to wield the sword, than to sweep the strings of the harp, which I have vowed never to touch until the holy city be restored to its former glory, and the base enemy be driven from before the shrine. Where once all was sacred, they have builded temples of worship to their idols, and altars to the tyrant Antiochus. My right arm has smitten the unfaithful, who dared worship at their shrines. Many true hearted sons of Israel rose up in arms and destroyed the profaned altars. And I and some others were forced to flee the city.

DEBORAH: The Lord has been merciful in guiding thee safely to Modin.

DAVID: O mother, all along the way mine eyes were a witness to the evil work of the enemy. Nothing but fire and blood greeted my sight during the past few weeks. Even now, as I wended my way to Modin, I received word of a terrible disaster. A thousand of our people have been cruelly slain in the wilderness, in cold blood, because they would not defile their Sabbath by resisting the enemy on that day. I can bear it no longer, and that is why I am here, for I came to join the camp of the Maccabees. Mother, dear mother, I know thou wilt not restrain me from so just a cause.

DEBORAH: My son, there is no greater pleasure in store for the heart of a true mother in Israel. But a while ago I pictured to myself how thou wouldst look in the martial garb of thy father. See, there lie his helmet and his sword. Take them. The Lord in his goodness has answered the fondest wishes of my heart in restoring thee to me, and now, dear son, thou mayest go to fight in His name. Yonder is the camp of the Maccabees. On those noble heights they defy the base enemy. Go! And, if it please the Lord, thou wilt return to me in victory. If not, I shall remember that it is the will of Him, who rules beyond the clouds.

Curtain.

Act I

SCENE I

The camp of the Maccabees. Mattathias and his five sons. Soldiers. Man on the ground before Mattathias.

MATTATHIAS *(Turning to Judas.):* Judas, what sayest thou shall be done with the culprit? It is almost a pity to put one like him to death, for he seems an able youth.

JUDAS: Ay, father, but consider, is he not a spy? Has he not taken steps to bring about our ruin, even risking his own life in the attempt to destroy our whole camp? What is the fate of all spies but death, and what other fate does he deserve?

MATTATHIAS: Thou sayest truly, my son. And yet it is not every soldier in the camp of Apollonius, who would undertake what this one has. And remember how bravely he bore himself when captured. I warrant me that without thy opportune arrival, he would have beaten our soldiers off. I cannot help but admire such bravery, and if it be possible, nothing would please me more than to spare his life. What say thy brothers on the matter? Speak, Jonathan and Simeon. What are your thoughts, John and Eleazar?

JOHN: Thy words, father, appear reasonable to me. This man should, if possible, be spared. But remember, father, he left the camp of Apollonius to bring about our destruction. How would his commander treat one of the Maccabees, if chance should ever throw him into his power?

SIMEON: My brother, I fear, is somewhat blinded by his hatred toward the enemy. What would we gain by the death of the culprit? He is in our power, and can do us no harm. While he lives he may do us good, for we can, perhaps, obtain from him valuable information.

(All nod in approbation.)

MATTATHIAS: Well spoken, my son. His tongue will, perhaps, save his life. We shall now see whether our captive will break his silence. *(Turning to spy, and touching him with his sword.)* Up! *(Spy rises and faces Mattathias.)*

MATTATHIAS: It were a pity to destroy thy life, my man, if it can possibly be spared. But whether thou livest or diest, rests now entirely with thee.

SPY: With me?

MATTATHIAS: Listen, and thou shalt see how. A few days ago I received word of the whereabouts of the enemy's camp. As yet I have sent no spy to learn its strength. There are two things which I desire to know, and these things I can obtain from thee. First, I desire to know, whether Apollonius intends to attack us soon. Then I wish to have a plan of the camp, so that I may send one of my men thither.

SPY: I am thy captive. I must bow to thy will.

MATTATHIAS: Then speak!

SPY: It is the intention of Apollonius to fall upon thee in about a fortnight. Early in the morning, he expects to surprise thy camp and demolish it completely. His plans are all made, though he has not yet decided upon the day. As to our camp, it is situated in a valley that is well guarded by sentinels, who hold all entrances to the neighborhood. Thou wilt find no difficulty, however, in passing our frontier lines on giving the countersign, which is "Apollonius, the Conqueror." Once within the lines, it is easy to obtain access to the tent of Apollonius by applying as a servant to his Excellency.

MATTATHIAS: 'Tis well. But remember, if thy words prove false, thou shalt forfeit thy life. *(Turning to Judas.)* Bring David to me. *(To spy.)* I shall send into thy camp one whom I value highly, for a braver lad the entire Syrian host does not contain. If thy story prove untrue, and they touch but a hair of his head as a consequence, remember— thou art in the hands of the Maccabees!

SPY: Would that I could feel as safe on the field of battle.

(Enter David and Judas.)

MATTATHIAS: Ah, David. I have an errand for thee, my lad, but it is a dangerous one. Thou art to go into the camp of the enemy, and learn when they are to attack us. Judas will instruct thee further. But, before thou goest, take this, a half of a drachma, broken by my sword. The other portion I hold. When the enemy is ready to fall upon us, contrive to send me thy portion the day before, and if it match the portion I have, I will know it to be a signal from thee that the enemy is about to attack us. And now go. *(Exit David.)* As for him, *(Indicating spy.)* guard him well. His fate hangs upon the words he has uttered. *(Spy led out R.)*

(Enter soldier in haste L.)

MATTATHIAS: What now, Reuben?

SOLDIER: O Mattathias! We have just discovered that one of our men has deserted. Azarias has gone off to join the Syrian host.

MATTATHIAS: What! A traitor in Israel? Go, seek him at once. Spare no effort to bring him back into the camp which he would disgrace. Go Judas! Simeon! John! Eleazar and Jonathan! Let him not escape us. Ten talents of silver to the man who brings him back, dead or alive.

Curtain.

Tent of Apollonius. Apollonius reclining on divan. Fool sitting on the floor in foreground. Alnashar. Soldiers and slaves.

ALNASHAR: Yes, your Excellency, there is no use in delaying the attack any longer. The Jews are very weak, and but few in number. We can easily destroy them and have done with them forever.

APOLLONIUS: So we can, indeed, and that with but a handful of men. I really think it unnecessary for more than a few chosen ones to make the attack. It would be flattering to them, to be sure, if the entire Syrian host were to march against a handful of Jews. Should the rogues be fortunate enough to repel our band, it will then be ample time to think seriously of them. In the meanwhile, hast thou made preparation for our return, and for the proper conveyance of the captives?

ALNASHAR: All is in readiness, your Excellency. We await but the order to attack. Our swords are thirsting for Jewish blood, and I know my hand, for one, is itching for the spoils.

APOLLONIUS: Didst thou say thirsting for Jewish blood? I have a blade here that shall drink most unsparingly. See, this sword I reserve for Judas Maccabaeus himself. Him I shall be courteous enough to slay with a gold-tipped blade. Such handles of inlaid ivory and pearl are not to be found in every camp. It is almost a pity to stain it with the caitiff's blood. No, I'll not. For him I'll have in store a more deserving fate. He shall share the lot of the women and children; but only at first. Then, when I have dragged him a captive in chains, from the Euphrates to the Nile, I'll permit one of my slaves to dispatch him. There are chains enough in the camp of Apollonius for the Maccabees and their entire band. *(Turning to soldier.)* Bring me of the fetters that lie without. *(Exit soldier.)* We'll see by tomorrow whether these fellows in chains will be as cheerful and as defiant as they are in the mountains. *(Enter soldier with chains.)* I warrant thee there will be quite a change in the atmosphere. *(To Fool.)* Come, fool, what sayest thou to these shackels? What thinkest thou, eh?

Will the lion of Modin roar when we twist his tad? Speak and mark that thy words be witty.

FOOL: Your Excellency, from what I have heard of this Judas, he *is* a lion—in the fight, but an eel in fetters. I fear me you will find him a slippery article indeed. And as for twisting" the lion's tail—rather your Excellency than I.

APOLLONIUS *(Angrily.):* Knave, What knowest thou of this Judas, and of eels?

FOOL: Naught but what hath reached these ears of mine, your Excellency.

APOLLONIUS: Those ears? And, pray, what have long ears like thine to do with such rumors? I fear me, thou hast been meddling out of thy profession. *(To Alnashar.)* Where didst thou say this knave was found?

ALNASHAR: Outside of the camp, your Excellency. He expressed a desire to serve thee, and hearing that thou wert in need of a jester, he volunteered to play the fool.

APOLLONIUS: Then he has not always been a fool. *(To Fool.)* Knave! *(Seeing the scar.)* But how comest thou by that scar over thy temple? Hast seen fighting?

FOOL: Your Excellency, fools are born, not made. That scar I received in a scuffle, but not by the sword. It chanced one day, that a wise thought had gone astray, and straggling toward my poor brain, attempted to enter my head, not knowing the density of my skull. The thought struggled to get in. My skull sought to keep it out, and as a result of the conflict, I bear the scar to witness.

APOLLONIUS: Ah! Well said again. Truly, knave, thy wit hath proved thy salvation this time, for I was about to order thee to be hung up by the heels, and not a morsel of food wouldst thou have had the entire day.

FOOL: O your Excellency! Hung by the heels?

APOLLONIUS: Yes, with thy head down. To a fool it matters little whether his feet be in the place of his head, or his head in place of his feet.

FOOL: In that case, your Excellency, it would also matter little, whether I partake of food or not.

APOLLONIUS: And why?

FOOL: 'Tis plain, your Excellency, that my stomach would then be far above my thoughts.

APOLLONIUS: Ah! Well said again. That was a clever one. Come, thou must have thy reward for this. Ask, and it shall be granted. But, remember, ask thou wisely, though boldly.

FOOL: For myself, your Excellency, I have nothing to ask. But, knowing how sad will be the fate of those who are unfortunate to be your enemies, it is for them that I would make a little request. And that is, to send them by your messenger—

APOLLONIUS: Ah! That reminds me. Alnashar, you are to go to the camp of the caitiffs at once, to deliver a message, giving them their last chance to surrender. *(To Fool.)* But knave, what wouldst thou with my messenger?

FOOL: Your Excellency, with thy permission and that or the noble Alnashar, I desire to send to the Jewish band this broken drachma— 'tis all I have in the world—as a token of my sympathy.

APOLLONIUS: Verily, a foolish request, and harmless withal. *(To Alnashar.)* Alnashar, take the coin. And now, knave, have done with thee. Away. *(Fool bows himself toward the door.)* No—stay a while. I am weary, and need more recreation. Canst perhaps entertain me in some other fashion? Dost play the harp?

FOOL: The harp! I have taken a vow, that these hands of mine shall never sweep its strings until—*(Pausing suddenly.)* until—

APOLLONIUS: Until what?

FOOL: Until I learn how to play.

APOLLONIUS: What! another jest? Enough for today. Away with thee! *(Exit Fool.) (To Alnashar.)* And now for the message. Tell Judas that I give him three days' time in which to decide. If, at the end of three days, he does not surrender, I will destroy the camp and put to the sword every man, woman and child. That will put him off the track. Little will he think then that in the morning we are going to attack him. And mind—don't fail to deliver the fool's message. I warrant thee it will stir up their anger not a little to receive the sympathy of a fool. But stay—where is Azarias? *(To soldier.)* Tell Azarias to come hither. He knows the Jewish camp well. 'Tis but a few days since he left the Maccabees to join our camp, and he can be of great service to us. Under his direction I shall make the attack, and under his guidance, I have no doubt, thou wilt reach the place in safety.

(Enter Azarias and soldier.)

AZARIAS: Your Excellency.

APOLLONIUS: Azarias, Alnashar is to go into the camp of the Maccabees, bearing a message from me, and I have chosen thee to guide him. Thou knowest the roads well.

AZARIAS: Yes, your Excellency. There is but one narrow and dangerous pass that leads to the camp, and if we make haste, we can return before night.

APOLLONIUS: Then go at once. *(Exit Alnashar. Azarias remains.)* Why dost thou linger?

AZARIAS: Your Excellency, I have something to tell thee. As I was coming to thy door, there came from within this tent a man whom I suspect as—

APOLLONIUS: What! A spy in this camp? Name him.

AZARIAS: I am not certain, your Excellency. But I fear there is an enemy here in the guise of a fool.

APOLLONIUS: What! My fool?

AZARIAS: Yes, your Excellency. It seems that I have seen him somewhere before. I am not certain just where, for it is rather difficult to recognize one in such a garb. But that scar on his temple looks familiar.

APOLLONIUS: Nonsense. It is mere fancy on your part. He is nothing but a harmless fool, and has proven himself such. Would that all mine enemies were as harmless as he. Now, leave me. Alnashar is awaiting thee. Hasten upon thine errand, and do not fail to return before night. Tomorrow, at sunrise, we shall be ready. And now, I must go to prepare for the attack. *(Exit R., Azarias exit L.)*

Curtain.

ACT II

SCENE I

The tent of Judas Maccabaeus. Judas, Jonathan, soldiers.

JUDAS: What news of the traitor, brother Jonathan?

JONATHAN: None, brother Judas. He is gone. We have searched every piece of ground in the direction of the enemy's camp, but found no trace of him. I fear we were too late. He had too great a start and must have been with the enemy, when the news of his desertion reached us. We looked and looked for days, but in vain. *(Enter John.)*

JUDAS: Here is John. I see thou, too, hast found no trace of him.

JOHN: None whatever, brother Judas, nor have our brothers, Eleazar and Simeon. They, too, have returned without the traitor.

JUDAS: Ah! 'Tis a pity. The coward should have been brought to me. Oh! If I only have the good fortune to meet him in battle! *(Enter soldier.)*

SOLDIER: A messenger has arrived from the camp of Apollonius and desires to enter.

JUDAS: Bring him in. *(Exit soldier.)* No doubt some insolent message from the haughty Apollonius.

(Enter Alnashar, blindfolded, between two soldiers.)

JUDAS: Remove the bandage. *(Bandage raised.)* And now, what is thy pleasure, Syrian?

ALNASHAR: I come to deliver a message from my master, Apollonius.

JUDAS: Speak.

ALNASHAR: The noble Apollonius has sent me thither to ask thee to surrender. He gives the Maccabees three days' grace. If, at the end of that time, thou refusest to capitulate as prisoners of war, and to become slaves to his majesty, Antiochus, Apollonius will attack the camp and put every man, woman and child to the sword.

JUDAS *(With a sneer.)*: Is that all?

ALNASHAR: That is all, and I can assure thee that none will be spared. Thou needest expect no mercy, for there is not a grain of sympathy for the Maccabees in our ranks. Stay—yes, I had almost forgotten. There is one, who has shown some feeling for you all, and he is no other than the jester of Apollonius, who sends a fool's offering in the shape of a coin.

ALL *(With significant glances.):* A coin!

ALNASHAR *(Fumbling in his girdle for it.)*: Yes, a coin. I had it but a while ago. Ah! Here it is. See, it is but a broken one at that.

JUDAS *(Hastily seizing the coin.)*: 'Tis well. Tell thy master, that Judas thanks him most heartily for allowing some sympathy, even if it be only that of a fool. Tell him that we all thank him for it, and that we appreciate it fully. As for his empty threat to put us all to the sword, tell him the Maccabees will consider it a pleasure to meet him on the field of battle. Then it will be seen with whom it rests to be lavish of mercy.

ALNASHAR: Then thou dost not comply? Wilt still hold out?

JUDAS: Comply? Never! And now not another word. Go.

(Aln., blindfolded again, is led out by two soldiers.)

JUDAS *(Turning to brothers.)*: See! David still lives. It is from him—the fool of Apollonius. *(Takes the other part from girdle and matches it.)* Yes. It is from David, for the part fits.

JONATHAN: Then Apollonius will attack us tomorrow.

JUDAS: Yes, early in the morning, and the wretch sent word that he gives us three days' time. We must act at once. Go, brother Jonathan. Give word that John and Simeon are to guard the rear of the camp with their men, whilst thou and Eleazar repair to the sides, and stand ready to meet the enemy at sunrise. *(To soldiers.)* Go, my men, make haste. I ' ill protect the frontier with my chosen band. Quickly, there is not a moment to be lost.

Curtain.

SCENE II

Syrian soldiers seen running, some of them exclaiming: "Run for your lives! Run! The Jews are behind us!" etc. Among them is Azarias, who comes staggering on the scene. Soldiers hurrying by shout: "Run for thy life, Azarias!"

AZARIAS: Not another step will I go today. *(Seats himself on rock.)* Run, indeed. Well, all the good running will do them. For my part, I'd just as lief die here as die running I've run enough today, and I don't care if Judas Maccabaeus himself comes after me. I won't budge another inch. Oh *(Shaking his head dolefully.)* all this comes from not taking my advice. I told Apollonius we could expect nothing good from that fool. A harmless fool, he called him. *(Sarcastically.)* Harmless. He wished that all his enemies were as harmless. Well, they are. I have never, in all my life, seen a harmless man do so much damage in one day.

(Enter Aln. running. He stops on seeing Az.)

ALNASHAR: Azarias! In the name of the great Antiochus, what art thou doing here? Why dost thou not run for thy life?

AZARIAS: Doing? Why, I'm doing the same thing here, that I'd be doing there. *(Pointing in direction in which soldiers ran.)* It's just as near to heaven here as it is there. There's no use in trying to run away from death, especially when death is working for the Maccabees. Oh, it's all up. We're done for—surrounded on every side, and thou mayest as well keep me company to the golden shore when the time comes.

ALNASHAR: Why, what dost thou mean?

AZARIAS: Mean? What can I mean? Canst not see how badly beaten we are, not the least chance to escape? And it's all because Apollonius wouldn't listen to me.

ALNASHAR: Come, come. Don't try to lay the blame on anybody. It's neither thou, nor I, nor Apollonius, who is at fault. It's merely the strong arm of Judas Maccabaeus and his brothers. My! But I never saw such action in all my days. They made us fly like chaff before the wind. I do assure thee that if I had had any idea of what fighters these Maccabees were, I would have stayed at home. But what's the use of worrying? It's all over and poor Apollonius! That gold-tipped sword of his, which seemed so thirsty for blood, has had its fill—but not of *Jewish* blood. Judas Maccabaeus has been keeping it at work pretty busily with his powerful arm, and Apollonius ought to be glad he's no longer alive to see what a wreck his army has become. There's no use of worrying, I say. Come, brace up, Azarias. Thou seemest blue. All isn't lost yet. Look here. *(Holds out flask.)* Here's my last resort—a good friend in need, I can tell thee. I'm just going to take a drop to cheer me up, and drown my sorrows. *(Drinks.)* Here *(Offers it to Asanas.)* It's good stuff. Excellent wine of ten years' vintage.

AZARIAS *(Ignoring the offer and holding his head down.)*: I told him, but he wouldn't heed my words. Thought he knew it all. When I told him that fool looked suspicious, he said he was harmless. And I have never seen a harmless man fight like that in all my life.

(Alnashar, looking toward the left, suddenly gets scared, drops his flask, and quietly sneaks away, leaving Azarias alone, who continues without looking up) :

I tell thee, Alnashar, I have never liked the looks of that fool.

(Enter fool running. He stops on seeing Azarias; quietly steals up behind him, and stands over him with drawn sword.)

O, if I could only fight the battle over again! If I only had my sword, I know what I'd do. This arm *(Holding it out before him.)* would do the work. There's only one man whom I'd wallop *(Shaking his fist.)* and I tell thee if I ever laid this on that fool *(Looks up, and seeing the fool, falls off the rock with surprise and fright. Begins rolling about the ground.)* I—I—oh—I—please don't—I—I—didn't meant it—I was only

FOOL: Silence, knave. Arise! *(Azarias arises.)* And so we have the traitor, at last. Come, Azarias, where is thy sword? Where is thy army? And

Apollonius, my master? Ha! Ha! What has become of him? Speak, why art thou silent?

(More soldiers arrive on the scene. Enter Judas, followed by soldiers.)

DAVID: Yes, I found him sitting here all alone, telling himself a story. It was all about Azarias, too. Azarias was telling Azarias what Azarias would do, if Azarias could only fight the battle over again.

(Enter Jewish soldier, crying:) "Here he is. Here is David." *(Seeing Azarias.)* "What? Azarias! Azarias, the traitor!"

JUDAS: David! We have been seeking thee, fearing that something had befallen. Whom have we here? Azarias! Ah, traitor! So it is thou, who hast required the attention of David. I fear he has been wasting time with thee. Better would he have done, had he slain thee at once, for death should be the punishment of one who raises his hand in strife against his own people.

(Enter Eleazar and Jonathan, bringing in Alnashar bound.)

Pray, whom have we here, brothers?

JONATHAN: This, if thou remember, brother Judas, is the messenger, who dared to utter insolent words in our camp.

ELEAZAR: We found him running, for he knew of thy approach, and that is how we learned that you were all here.

JUDAS: Here is a fitting companion for him. Let them both be bound together and marched to our camp. And now, what news of the enemy in that direction?

ELEAZAR: There is no news, brother Judas, for there is no enemy. Besides a few carcasses of elephants, there are but the remains of the slain Syrian host scattered here and there.

JUDAS: Then our victory is complete. The Lord has been with us, and the cause of the Maccabees has triumphed again. *(Praying.)*: O Lord,

Thou who hast smitten the enemies of Israel in Egypt, who hast delivered the army of the Philistines into the hands of Saul and David, who hast put down the enemies of thy people. Thou hast once more smitten the enemy with Thy right hand. Blessed art Thou, O Savior of Israel. Let all that know Thy name praise thee with thanksgiving and song.

Curtain.

Act III

Alnashar and Azarias, bound together, sitting on the ground.

ALNASHAR: Well, we're in a nice fix now, and I wonder how much longer this sort of thing is going to last.

AZARIAS: O, don't mention it. I'm sick and tired. Every time I think of it I get the blues. O, if I could only get loose. To be dragged around like this, day after day, week after week, and month after month, is enough to make anybody disgusted with life.

ALNASHAR: O, there's no kick coming from thee. Be glad thou'rt alive. Why, thou never didst expect to live another day!

AZARIAS: I didn't. It's true. But that's no reason why thou shouldst have run away and left me when thou sawest that fool coming. I tell thee, if I had only been sure that he was David of Modin, when he played the fool in the camp of poor Apollonius, he'd never have lived to stand over me with sword in hand, I tell thee that.

ALNASHAR: Now, look here. Thou hast lost nothing, after all, by remaining and I didn't gain anything by running away. They caught me anyhow.

AZARIAS: So they did, and they attached thee to me.

ALNASHAR: Well, I don't like this partnership any more than thou, but as long as we're together we may as well be cheerful and make the best of it. Come, let's walk around a bit. I'm beginning to feel stiff in the limbs.

AZARIAS: No! Sit where you are. I'm tired.

ALNASHAR: There thou art again. Every time I want to walk, thou desirest to rest, and every time I want to sit down, thou gettest a notion to go strutting about. Now, please understand that half of these chains are mine, and I've got as much to say as thou hast. So there. *(Jumps up, dragging Az. with him.)*

AZARIAS: See here. Dost forget that the other half belong to me? As far as I'm concerned, thou canst have my share of the chains, too. But thou needest not have thy way all the time.

ALNASHAR: Come, now, Azarias. Let us not quarrel. We ought to sympathize with each other. Here we are left alone, while they are fighting on all sides of us. We're doomed to sit quietly and watch them cut our armies all to pieces. I wonder how today's battle will end. Perhaps Lysias will put an end to these Maccabees, and then we'll be free.

AZARIAS: Thou wonderest. Well, there's no more possibility of the Maccabees losing this battle than that Apollonius will come to life again. Why, Lysias doesn't stand any more chance than a fly. See! There go his soldiers, scattering for dear life. Why, their own elephants are trampling them under foot. Another victory for Judas and his band.

ALNASHAR: Yes, and this time I'm afraid they'll get Jerusalem back. See! They're coming this way, marching triumphantly. Good-bye to all our hopes. Lysias is defeated. No liberty for us. We'll have to be their slaves, go with them to Jerusalem and do all the dirty work.

AZARIAS: Well, we won't be the only ones, that's certain. I can see that by the number of captives they're bringing with them.

(Cries of "Judas Maccabaeus! Long live the Maccabees!" Soldiers march in with captives. Judas and brothers, David. Cries of "Judas! Long live Judas Maccabaeus!")

JUDAS: My friends, ye who have fought so nobly today, do me great honor, more than I deserve, I fear. The God of Israel has been with us today, and has spread havoc among our enemies. This victory is due to you all, as well as to me. But let us not forget one who has done so much for us, and who has always been among the foremost in our battles. Let us ever remember that we owe much of our victory to that brave youth, David of Modin.

(Cries of "Long live David! David of Modin!")

And now there remains but one thing more for us to do. Our enemies are driven before us. They, who have opposed the children of Israel, and have destroyed our Temple, fear us. The host of the tyrant Antiochus are no more. Let us complete the good work. Our Temple remains desecrated. The city of Jerusalem waits to receive us. The days when its enemies dwelt therein are gone. Let us now advance and build up the holy city once more. Let us march on to Jerusalem.

(Cries of "To Jerusalem! On to Jerusalem!")

Hanukkah Evening

Room with table set for supper. On a small stand to one side a candelabrum. Mother and two children, boy and girl. Mother in rocker, sewing. Children studying, the one with book, the other with slate.

HYMAN: Mother, this is a very hard lesson. I can't do this arithmetic and I won't try. Miss Smith, my teacher, is too mean, anyway.

MOTHER: My dear little boy, you are not losing your patience too son? I am sure that Miss Smith does not treat little boys meanly. If she seems mean to you, it may be that *you* are to blame. People often seem to us what we are to them. Try to please Miss Smith, and I am sure that she will please you. Don't lose patience over your lessons. If once or twice, you don't succeed, try, try, again.

FANNY *(Going to Mother with a book.)*: Mother, what is this word?

MOTHER: *Festival.* It is quite a big word for a little girl isn't it? A festival is a happy time, such as our *Hanukkah* is.

FANNY: Oh! I wish that papa would come soon so that he could light the candles! *(Footsteps heard outside.)*

HYMAN: Ah! There comes papa. *(He jumps up, runs to meet him, and comes in, holding him by the hand. Fanny goes to meet him. He enters and kisses her, then kisses Mother, saying)*: Mamma, dear! Were you worried?

MOTHER: Yes, papa, you are late tonight.

FATHER: I could not get home sooner, my dear, but I am so much gladder to be here now.

MOTHER: Supper has been waiting for you half an hour.

FATHER: We shall soon have it now, but first let us do our duty to God and kindle the *Hanukkah* lights.

CHILDREN: O yes, O yes, do!

FATHER *(Wife and children gathered around him, kindles the light, saying the following benediction.)*: Blessed be Thou, O Lord our God, Ruler of the world, who hast kept us alive to this day, who hast sanctified us with Thy commandments, and hast enabled us to kindle the *Hanukkah* lights.

MOTHER: And now let us have supper.

(Father and children go to table. Mother goes out, but returns at once, bearing tray with coffee pot and dishes of food, places things on the table and takes her seat. At Father's place is a loaf of bread.)

HYMAN: Gee, papa, but I'm hungry!

FATHER: I suppose so, but we must first make *Motze. (Prayer over the bread.) (Says the following benediction, cuts the loaf of bread and gives each a piece.)* We bless and praise Thee, O Lord our God, Ruler of the world, for Thou has enriched us with the products of the earth.

(They begin to eat. On lifting up, their plates, Hyman and Fanny discover money. Both exclaim, holding up the coins.) Hello! What's this?

FATHER: That's *Hanukkah-Geld*. This is a time when we must all be happy, and I know that some spending money will make my little boy and girl happy.

HYMAN: Thank you, papa dear.

(Fanny runs up and kisses papa.)

MOTHER: Papa, why were you late this evening?

FATHER *(Smiling.)*: Such curiosity. *Must* you know everything? As if I were so important that every moment of my life is worth knowing about!

MOTHER: It *is* important to me, papa dear.

FATHER: Well, if you *must* know, I will tell you, although it is one of those things which are better if not spoken about, but you must promise me not to scold.

MOTHER: Very well. It is *Hanukkah* tonight, and I suppose we'll have to be pleasant, whether we want to or not. Still, I hope it was nothing so very bad that kept you away.

FATHER: Well, we'll see. When I left the shop, I went to take the car for home. The distance, you know, is great, and it was too late for me to walk. As I approached the corner where I was to board the car, I noticed an old woman trudging slowly along, carrying a heavy bundle. When I came up to her, she stopped me and said: 'Will you please tell me how far it is yet to Henry street.' I told her it was a long distance. I noticed that she was aged, weary and poor. I told her that she had better ride. She said that she wished that she could, but he had come down town to buy a few things where she could get them a little cheaper, and after paying for them, found that she had no money left, and concluded to walk home. She soon found this to be beyond her strength. I put my hand into my pocket and discovered to my surprise that I had only one nickel left. Some other little change that I had I left with you this morning to put under the children's plates at supper for *Hanukkah-Geld*. What was I to do? I was late as it was. Still, I hadn't the heart to forsake that poor, feeble, unfortunate old woman. I thought, better that *I* should walk and be late that that *she* should, and I begged her to permit me to put her on the car. With a grateful look she consented, expressing the hope that God would bless me for my kindness to an old lady. I put her on the car and handed her fare to the conductor. I was penniless. The only thing that remained for me to do was to walk home. I did so, running part of the way for fear that you would be worried. And this is why I was late.

MOTHER *(Smiling.)*: And for this you thought that I would *scold* you? If you hadn't assisted the old lady, I *should* have scolded you. You know that our religion teaches loving kindness and charity, and that we are commanded in the Scriptures to respect the aged and help the poor. The *Hanukkah* lights will always shine more brightly for us if we make the lives of others brighter and happier. And you, my children, let me ask you always to remember as a *Hanukkah* lesson that God makes those happy who gives happiness to others. The old lady hoped that God would bless papa. And so he did. Her prayer is already fulfilled. Are we not all happier for the kindness papa did?

(The children together.) Yes, mamma dear.

FATHER: And now I want to know how my little boy and girl got along today at school?

HYMAN: What do you think papa, I was put at the head of the class!

FATHER: Really?

FANNY: Papa, you know that Hym's class had two heads. Ed. Jones was put at one head and Hyman at the other. *(All laugh except Hyman, who pouts.)*

MOTHER *(Looking at the Hanukkah lights.)*: How beautifully those little lights shine. They look like little messengers of joy from on high.

FATHER: They are, Mother, to turn our thoughts toward heaven.

FANNY: Papa, what does *Hanukkah* mean anyhow?

FATHER: Well, I shall tell you.

(Fanny and Hyman jump up from table, eager to hear.)

FATHER: One minute, let us first say grace. After we have eaten and enjoyed God gifts, it is only proper that we should thank Him. Therefore our religion teaches: Thou shalt eat, satisfy thyself and thank God. So let us say a word of grace.

(Fanny and Hyman sit down again.)

FATHER *(All bow heads.)*: We give thanks to Thee, O Lord, our God, Ruler of the world, for the bounties we enjoy at this table. May we try to live so as to be worthy of Thy love. Blessed be Thou, O God, who feedest all Thy creatures. Amen!

(All leave table except Mother, who remains seated. Father takes rocker. Children sit about him as he tells story of Hanukkah.)

FATHER: And now, my children, I shall tell you the wonderful story of *Hanukkah. Hanukkah* reminds us of something that took place over 2,000 years ago. The Jewish people then lived in a country called Palestine. There came a cruel king of Syria, Antiochus Epiphanes, to make war upon them. He desired to do away wit' the Jews. He hated them and their religion. He tried to prevent them from worshipping God. He spoiled their beautiful and sacred temple. Then arose an old Jewish man, Mattathias, in defense of his people. He and his five sons raised an army to oppose the Syrians. Soon Mattathias died. His bravest son, Judas the Maccabee, as he was later called, became leader of the people. For three years he and his army fought against the greater armies of the Syrians. At last Judah Maccabee conquered. He drove the enemy out of Jerusalem and Palestine. He then purified and rededicated the temple. In the temple was found a little bottle of oil, which was just enough for one day, for the perpetual light which burns before the ark, wherein is kept the Torah. But when it was lighted, wonderful to tell, it burned eight days! We kindle our *Hanukkah* lights for eight days to remind us of these wonderful events in the history of our people.

FANNY: I don't understand, papa, how Judas Maccabee and his small army could have overcome so many enemies.

FATHER: He did, my children, because God was on his side. As long as God is with us we need not fear. No one can do us real harm. *Hanukkah* is a proclamation of God's wondrous power to help his trusting children.

HYMAN: Papa, don't you remember that last year we sang such a beautiful *Hanukkah* song?

FATHER: Yes, my dear; shall we sing it now?

CHILDREN: Yes, do.

FATHER: Very well, let us all sing it together.

(They chant the Hanukkah Hymn—Union Hymnal—the school joining in.)

I. Rock of Ages, let our song
    Praise Thy saving power;
    Thou, amidst the raging foes,
       Wast our Shel'ring tower.
    Furious they assailed us,
    But Thin arm availed us,
       And Thy word
       Broke their sword
    When our own strength failed us.

II. Kindling fresh the holy lamps,
       Priests approved in suffering,
    Purified the nation's shrine,
       Brought to God their offering.
    And His court surrounding,
       Hear, in joy abounding,
       Happy throngs
       Singing songs
    With a mighty sounding.

III. Children of the Martyr-race,
       Whether free or fettered,
    Wake the echoes of the songs,
       Where ye may be scattered.
    Yours the message cheering
    That the time is nearing
       Which will see
       All men free,
    Tyrants disappearing.

Curtain.

THE SEVEN LIGHTS

DIRECTIONS: *Judah Maccabee is dressed in military costume. The seven lights, represented by girls, are dressed in loose costumes, each a different color. They take their places on the stage in a semi-circle. Each carries a candle in a fancy holder, flower shaped. Uncle Sam should be a small boy dressed in the regulation Uncle Sam costume. At one side of the stage should be a lighted candle on a small table, with which Judah kindles the different candles held by the girls.*

JUDAH: *(Standing in center of stage.)*
I represent the warrior bold
Before whose might, in days of old,
Brave Israel's Syrian foe was quelled
And from the holy shrine expelled.
For Israel was God's chosen son,
Sent forth to tell that God is One.
The Syrian sought to bring him low,
But God put forth the saving blow.
Through me and those who bled and died
Our shrine was saved and purified.
Remembering the glorious fight
We kindle now the Hanukkah light.
Behold the truths for which we fought;
These precious gems from heaven brought:
(Here Judah steps to side of stage.)
Fair Unity, I bid thee speak
They message out from peak to peak:

(Unity comes from behind the scenes and takes her place at center of stage. Judah lights the candle in her hand, retires to the side, and Unity speaks. This procedure is followed by each new speaker in turn.)

UNITY: The Unity of God I've told
Unto the world, from days of old;
It is all Israel's battlecry,
The Lord our God is One for aye.

JUDAH: How worship Him, the only One,
                  Whose love for us so much hath done?
                  Come forth, fair Righteousness, and tell
                  What He, the Lord of Hosts, loves well.

RIGHTEOUSNESS: Of him who seeks to gain His love
                   And bounteous blessings from above,
                   Our Father asks no other sign
                   Save that we do His will benign.

JUDAH: This earth would be a paradise,
                  If men would only harmonize;
                  Come forth and read, Fraternity,
                  Your message to humanity.

FRATERNITY: I teach, since God is One, Father of all,
                  Man should man his brother call.
                  All human creeds should only teach
                  That God is One and good to each.

JUDAH: But man with brother-man has fought
                  Because he differed in his thought.
                  O, Tolerance, bright angel say,
                  Is this, then, "walking in His way?"

TOLERANCE: Since God is One, the same to all,
                  United we must stand or fall.
                  The worship He accepts must be
                  Deep rooted in Humanity.

JUDAH: To ease life's trials, grief, distress
                  And bring back long-lost happiness
                  Thou, Charity, art sent abroad
                  By Him, the Everlasting God

CHARITY:	Sweet Charity, the noblest part
	Of every gentle, human heart,
	With sorrow walks and soothes and stills
	All mankind's many urgent ills.
	I furnish comfort, solace, rest
	Through me, Religion's highly blest.
JUDAH:	When all life's restlessness is past,
	And death the lot for us has cast,
	Is there no other hope that we
	Inherit Immortality?
IMMORTALITY:	I represent the afterlife
	The climax to this world of strife.
	I promise men great joys above,
	Where bides a Father's lasting love.
JUDAH:	To spread such truth did God decree,
	That Israel should the "chosen" be.
	What is the word which echoed o'er
	The universe in days of yore?
ISRAEL'S MISSION:	"Let there be light," the mandate spake;
	Its accents caused the earth to quake.
	To spread abroad a creed of light,
	Is Israel's duty and delight.
JUDAH:	The keynote of our creed sublime,
	Is this, 'twill linger through all time:
	Sh'ma Yisroel, Israel Hear!
	One is Thy God, without compeer.
	Let us with gladness this song sing,
	The world shall with its echo ring.

(Here the Sh'ma Yisroel is sung by the school. An appropriate musical setting can be found in the hymnals. As the song is closing, Uncle Sam walks in, taking his place opposite Judah, and says:)

What means this gathering here today?

JUDAH: We come in peace to sing and pray.

UNCLE SAM: Religion is a power for good;
Without it nations never stood.
Your faith ever shall welcome be,
Has it a kindly thought of me?

JUDAH: Dear Uncle Sam, the faith we claim
Does venerate your glorious name.
The love for you that in us dwells
In noble song from our heart swells.

(Here "America" is sung by the school. As the song draws to a close Judah and Uncle Sam walk to the center of the stage and clasp hands.)

Curtain.

A Maccabean Cure

CHARACTERS

PHILIP BECKMAN, aged twelve
MRS. PHILIP BECKMAN, his mother
BELLA, his aunt
MOLLY, his nurse
DOCTOR SLESIGNER, his physician
HARRY, "Menelaus"
SAMMY, "King Antichus"
HERBIE, "Mattathias"
CHARLIE, "Judas Maccabeaus" } his friends
MARK, "Simon"
ERNEST, "Johanan"
LOUIS, "Eleazar"
BERNIE, "Jonathan"

SCENE—*The pretty living room of Mrs. Philip Beckman, Homestead, Pa.*

TIME—*The eve before Hanukkah, the present.*

DISCOVERED AT RISE OF CURTAIN-
Philip, a pale-faced boy, lying on a couch, half-covered by a robe, left front. His mother standing next to him, with medicine bottle and spoon. On a chair beside Philip is Doctor Slesinger, whose hat and small medicine satchel lie on the floor beside him. Molly, Philip's withered old nurse, is fanning the sick boy devotedly. All around are scattered the appurtenances of a comfortable living room: plenty of chairs, an open fireplace, a transparent screen before the fire. Lamps are lit, and the scene is pretty and cozy.

DOCTOR SLESINGER: Yes, he has a little rise of temperature. You say he does not complain of any special pain, Mrs. Beckman?

MRS. BECKMAN *(Anxiously.)*: Not any more than usual. But he worries me a great deal, Doctor. For a long time now he has been pale and quiet.

DOCTOR SLESINGER *(Shaking his head.)*: He should be out playing like other boys. Philip, won't you tell the doctor what hurts you?

PHILIP: It doesn't hurt anywhere.

DOCTOR SLESINGER *(Feeling his chest, back, etc.)*: No pain at all? I must confess, the case puzzles me. How is his appetite, Mrs. Beckman?

MOLLY *(In a trembling, high-pitched voice.)*: O Doctor, no more'n a birdie. A little peck here and there. It's only when Molly brings him a big piece of chocolate cake that he wants to eat at all.

DOCTOR SLESINGER *(Smiling.)*: That sounds natural.

PHILIP: But I like chocolate cake.

MRS. BECKMAN: Yes, that's it! He nibbles what he likes—cake, candy, jam—but I can't get him to eat bread and butter.

DOCTOR SLESINGER: Sounds like a case of mother-love. I should advise a little stronger food than chocolate cake.

PHILIP *(Burying his head in the pillow and beginning to cry.)*: O—o—h!

MRS. BECKMAN *(Lovingly.)*: My darling! You're breaking mother's heart.

MOLLY: My love! Don't cry. Molly won't let them hurt you. *(Pleadingly to the doctor.)* Please don't tease my little lamb.

DOCTOR SLESINGER *(Out of patience.)*: If he were mine, he would have some treatment of the boot-strap variety. I wish I could persuade you, Mrs. Beckman—

MRS. BECKMAN: But, Doctor Slesinger, you know this isn't natural. Philip doesn't sleep right; he dreams dreadfully.

DOCTOR SLESINGER *(Shaking his head and smiling.)*: If he were older, I might say some love-affair, but who can conceal a secret sorrow at twelve? How about school? Is he interested, Mrs. Beckman?

MRS. BECKMAN *(Horrified.)*: Why, I don't send him to public school. Indeed not! Hundreds of children coming from Heaven knows where!

DOCTOR SLESINGER: Probably just what he needs. Hothouse flowers often wilt, my friend. At least they don't grow big like garden plants and vegetables.

MOLLY *(Excitedly, crooning over Philip.)*: Garden plants and vegetables! My pet, my love, my angel!

BELLA *(A sweet young girl, hurrying in, her prayer book under her arm.)*: Hello, folks! What! Our baby ill? *(Runs over and hugs Philip.)* My darling! And I thought Auntie was to be allowed to take him to Temple with her—

PHILIP: But—I—don't—want—to—go!

MRS. BECKMAN: I just sent for the doctor, Bella. You know Doctor Slesinger? *(They smile and bow.)* I was so worried about Philip!

BELLA: More than usually?

DOCTOR SLESINGER: I admit, he puzzles me too, Miss Bella. I can't find a pain or an ache.

MOLLY: In a minute our doctor will be sending him to school, along with the riffraff and everyday boys.

BELLA: But that's where he ought to be. Haven't I always said so? O Doctor, I do wish you would be firm and tell my sister that precious little Philip should be up and doing with other children.

PHILIP *(Slowly.)*: But—I—*want*—to—go—to—school.

BELLA *(Delightedly.)*: You hear him, Lottie, you hear for yourself. Don't you see it's foolish to keep your angel wrapped in cotton wool?

MRS. BECKMAN *(Firmly.)*: My baby shall not go to school, nor to Sunday school either. I cannot afford to let my only child run the risk of contagious diseases and bad habits. You both know what ordinary boys attend the Homestead schools.

BELLA: Yes, *real boys*, with real *blood* in their veins.

DOCTOR SLESINGER: You're right, Miss Bella, quite right.

MRS. BECKMAN: But I teach him everything, every day at home. I give him Sunday school and Bible lessons most carefully myself.

DOCTOR SLESINGER: All of which does not include child companions. Mrs. Beckman, I begin to see why your little boy is pale and listless.

PHILIP *(Listlessly.)*: The—other—day—Sammy and Charlie—and I— we played Indians. We had a battle with Daniel Boone and Ouster and George Washington and—and Abraham Lincoln.

DOCTOR SLESINGER *(Delightedly.)*: Wrong on the dates, but right in the spirit. Mrs. Beckman, that is all your boy needs. Normal companionship, even though he should come home with a dirty face and a bump on his nose.

MOLLY *(Tragically.)*: A bump on his nose!

MRS. BECKMAN: I'm afraid I can't follow your prescription, Doctor. My boy is already too imaginative, and those boys might someday lead him into a serious adventure.

BELLA *(Picking up prayer book and muff.)*: I give it up, Lottie. If you refuse to see that we are living in a real world, that your boy is only a real boy, and that, worst of all, you are cheating him out of his real youth—the case is almost hopeless.

PHILIP: I'm so hungry—I want some chocolate cake.

MOLLY *(Hurrying out.)*: Wait, darling, Molly will get it for you.

DOCTOR SLESINGER *(Snapping his satchel shut.)*: I'm afraid I shall have to give up the case, Mrs. Beckman, until you are more willing to listen to reason. First, there is nothing the matter with your boy but a bad case of "spoiling," and secondly, I advise you strongly that he needs boys of his own age, not ladies, as companions.

MRS. BECKMAN *(Softly, but with determination.)*: I'm afraid, Doctor, I cannot agree that that is the cause of the trouble.

BELLA: Well, sister, you are coming to temple anyway. Philip is no worse than usual, in fact, a bit better. Come, Lottie. I'm sure that the calm and peace of the synagogue will prove to you that the doctor is quite right.

MRS. BECKMAN *(Putting on hat and coat, sadly.)*: Of course, I don't want to miss service on Hanukkah but, Doctor—

DOCTOR SLESINGER: I can only say, Mrs. Beckman, that your boy needs the tonic of human nature—some stirring interest, either real or imaginative.

MRS. BECKMAN *(Shaking her head; goes over to Molly to give directions.)*: Molly, now remember, toast and jam—*(Continues to give orders quietly, while Doctor Slesinger and Bella talk together.)*

DOCTOR SLESINGER: Seriously, Miss Bella, I wish we could get the boy away from here for a while.

BELLA: If only his father had lived, there would not have been this petticoat rule. *(A trifle mischievously.)* But don't give up, Doctor, I've a trick or two up my sleeve.

DOCTOR SLESINGER: What do you mean?

BELLA *(Whispering.)*: Tonight, after we're gone, there will be some happenings around here.

DOCTOR SLESINGER: Nothing dangerous?

BELLA: O, no, I'm not so foolish. Just some real boys, who know how to live in the past as well as the present. *(As Mrs. Beckman turns towards them.)* S—s—sh—! Won't you order that Philip should stay here, in this room? Say you like the surroundings, anything—

DOCTOR SLESINGER *(Nodding "yes.")*: Ready, Mrs. Beckman? I'm going too. I advise leaving Philip here on the couch. He seems a bit drowsy, and I'll look in on him again after temple.

MRS. BECKMAN *(As she kisses Philip lovingly.)*: Very well, Doctor. Molly, you will take the best of care of my darling?

BELLA: Hurry, dear, I fear we have already missed the opening hymn! You don't know how much I love going to the temple. I look forward to it all week.

Doctor Slesinger: I too. And I am particularly fond of this holiday. Come, Mrs. Beckman, we're waiting.

Mrs. Beckman *(Reluctantly, at the door.)*: Goodbye, darling! Mother will be home soon.

Philip *(Droopingly.)*: Bye—bye—

(They all exit.)

Molly *(Bustling around, lowering lights, fire, etc.)*: By-baby bunting, mother's gone a—

Philip *(Disgustedly.)*: Aw, I'm no girl-boy!

Molly: My darling, Nursie will get you some more chocolate cake.

Philip *(Lying down, disgustedly.)*: O, everybody makes such a baby out of me—. I wish I could play Buffalo Bill or Jesse James or—

Molly: Klotchly-klotchly! Where does he hear such talk?

Philip *(Burying his head in the pillow.)*: If I can't do anything else, I'll go to sleep and dream of them.

Molly: Duckie, old Molly'll fix you nice. *(She covers him up. He sinks into a restless sleep. Molly gets out her knitting, and sits before the fire. In a little while she too dozes, and soon sinks into a deep sleep. Shortly afterwards, Harry, Louis, Sammy, Herbie, Charlie, Mark, Ernest, and Bernie steal in quietly. They wear heavy overcoats, scarcely concealing costumes beneath.)*

Harry *(Whispering.)*: Think it's all right, fellows? Miss Bella, she made me promise to go ahead whatever happened.

Louis: Sure—but, look, he's asleep! And his nurse too—a big boy like him to have a *nurse*!

SAMMY: 'Tain't his fault. He'd like to play with us—it's his ma. Why, she don't even let him go to Sunday school to his *dear Aunt Bella!*

HERBIE: You better not talk about Miss Bella! I think she's great!

CHARLIE: You ain't the only one. Why'd we come here tonight, if it wasn't for her?

MARK: Let's get started. You fellows know your parts? I'm not so dead sure about mine.

ERNEST *(Braggingly.)*: I could say mine backwards—in the middle of the night.

BERNIE: You've got a cinch part.

LOUIS: I don't know; I'd rather be anybody than old Antiochus. Wasn't he fierce?

SAMMY *(Proudly.)*: Judas puts an end to him all right. Come, boys, let's start up.

(They take off their overcoats quietly, disclosing Sammy as Antiochus in kingly robes, Harry as Menelaus, the high priest, and the other boys in the worn, ragged costumes of the Maccabees.)

MARK: Isn't it awful to have to act here without scenery? It's going to be simply grand in Sunday school. *(Announcing dramatically.)* First Scene: Jerusalem, "Menelaus and Antiochus." Second Scene: Modin, "Mattathias and His Five Sons." Third Scene: Tabae, "Death-bed of Antiochus."

BERNIE *(Longingly.)*: I wish I was Judas! He's got 'em all beat a mile.

PHILIP *(Sitting up suddenly.)*: I can't keep quiet any longer! Say, what's all this? *(Looks at Molly.)* She'll be awake in a minute, and that'll be the end. Let's take her into the next room. You help, boys, and it'll be easy.

Louis: Who wants a *nurse* anyway?

(They all together lift the chair deftly and easily, and in a minute have hustled Molly, still sleeping, into the next room.)

Philip *(Running back to the sofa, delightedly.)*: Do hurry, boys, because mamma'll be home any minute, and that'll be the end of it all.

Harry: All right, we'll hustle. We're only glad you'll let us. See, we got to get this play in shape by Sunday, and nobody's got a house big enough to practice in.

(They look at each other sheepishly, as if anxious to keep a secret.)

Philip: O, I'm crazy to see the play. I don't think mamma would take me.

Charlie: Come, fellows, you're out of the first part. Just Harry and Sammy. Curtain rises on them, you know.

Philip: You can wait in the next room, if you want to, till your turn.

Bernie: No, sir, we can't afford to miss a word.

(They all group themselves around Philip on the couch, while Harry and Sammy take their positions, center stage.)

King Antiochus *(Sammy) (Sammy sitting stiffly on a high-backed chair, Menelaus bowing before him.)*: Come hither, Menelaus, I would confer with thee anent the Judeans.

Menelaus *(Harry)*: I pray, your Majesty, I would not trouble your Highness with the errors of your unfaithful subjects.

Antiochus *(Angrily.)*: Unfaithful again, you say? There shall be an end to them. I have enough of this treason.

Menelaus: Yes, your Majesty, they mock and scoff at you!

ANTIOCHUS: They mock at me, you say? They preach rebellion from Jerusalem? *(Strutting up and down.)* I shall teach them a pretty lesson. I shall pour the blood of unclean animals upon their altars and their sacred vessels!

MENELAUS *(Rubbing his hands gleefully.)*: But no! Deliver them to me, your Majesty. I shall make them give up their Torah, their Jewish rites and customs. Your Majesty, they mock at me too. I hate them as much as you do.

ANTIOCHUS: But I can trust you, Menelaus? Many dogs of Jews have betrayed their kings before now.

MENELAUS: Did I not steal the treasures of the temple for your Majesty? Have I not already delivered your enemies into your hands, the Hasidim and the Judeans? And today I have a most elaborate plan—

ANTIOCHUS *(Sitting in pensive thought.)*: What is it, Menelaus? Nothing can be too violent for these traitors. My wish is to exterminate them, to wipe them out completely. My mercenaries await my word, my troops will go over the kingdom destroying the infidels.

MENELAUS *(Cunningly.)*: Ah, your Majesty! But why destroy them, when we can make of them good Greek subjects? They will not give up their lives for their religion. You have merely to send your soldiers with the torch to their homes; you will soon see them give up their faith.

ANTIOCHUS: Would that I could believe you! But you are high priest, priest of the temple in Jerusalem. Why should I believe that you would truly change the religion of your followers? Most probably you will deliver me over to them.

MENELAUS: Ah! But, your Majesty, I desire to be high priest in the temple of the *Greeks*, and have hundreds, nay, thousands of followers. Give me the power to command your mercenaries, and in one month I shall have every Jew in your kingdom a good and loyal Greek.

ANTIOCHUS *(Extending his scepter.)*: I give you the power, Menelaus. Your life will be the forfeit, if I find that you commit any act of treachery and betray me to my enemies. The wicked Jews shall be made to bow before the great god Zeus. Their homes shall be ransacked, their temple destroyed, yea, even their Holy of holies shall reek with the fat of swine. And you, Menelaus, you shall do it, you the councillor, the friend, the help of Antiochus, shall become the high priest of the Greeks!

MENELAUS *(Dropping upon one knee.)*: Your Majesty, I thank you! Once again I shall have the chance to serve you. Once again I shall taste power and glory! And *(rising)* the temple of the god Zeus shall be crowded, the throng of Jews shall not worship the Almighty. I shall see their faces respond to the call of our trumpets. Judaism shall perish, and Antiochus shall be king of the world.

ANTIOCHUS: And Menelaus his prime minister! *(Laying his hand upon his shoulder.)* One word I would say to thee—beware of Judas!

MENELAUS *(Fiercely.)*: Death to Judas and the Hasmoneans!

SAMMY *(Taking off his crown, and going over to the boys.)*: I guess I didn't do a thing to those lines. Didn't know I could do 'em so well myself.

PHILIP *(Wistfully.)*: It was grand! If I could only be in it! Is Antiochus really going to do all that to the poor Jews?

HARRY *(Laughing.)*: No, no! It's all a play, but *(seriously)* it was much worse than that. We kids ought to be mighty glad we didn't live in those days.

CHARLIE *(Rising proudly.)*: Wait till you see my part! I'm the *hero*! I'm *Judas*! I'm the whole show! Say, Phil, do you know your mamma and all the rest of the people are at temple tonight just because of what I did thousands of years ago?

HERBIE *(Putting on a white wig.)*: Well, I like that! Don't you think Mattathias had some little thing to do with it?

MARK: And I may be only Simon, but I helped too. I guess we'd all better get a move on, or the Hanukkah services will be over!

(Herbie, Mark, Ernest, Louis, and Bernie all go to stage center. Herbie, weak and faltering, sits in the chair, while the others, except Charlie, group themselves about. Charlie waits a little to one side.)

MATTATHIAS *(Herbie)*: Alas, my sons! We have fallen upon troublous times! The hand of the betrayer is turned against us. You must avenge the God of your fathers.

SIMON *(Mark)*: But, alas, we have no armies! You, our fathers, have spent your strength. The hand of Menelaus, the high priest, is turned against us, we dare not worship in the temple.

JOHANAN *(Ernest)*: It is only yesterday that Lysias himself, once a friend of Menelaus, but now flown to the altar for protection, was slain in the house of God. Alas! What can we do when our own priest has turned against us?

ELEAZAR *(Louis)*: And they say in Jerusalem that Menelaus will stop at nothing. He plans to convert all the Jews to the Greek religion, and Antiochus has promised to make Menelaus priest of his own temple.

JONATHAN *(Bernie)*: And they have found out our haunts in the hills. We must seek new fighting grounds. We can no longer fight from ambush.

MATTATHIAS: You must not despair, my sons. The great God of Israel watches over all His children. Antiochus shall not conquer while Mattathias and his five sons live to carry the shield of the Almighty.

JONATHAN: Alas, father, we have no prophet in Israel! If we but had an Isaiah among us! Then we could rejoice and be stout of heart.

MATTATHIAS *(Rising and speaking in a trembling voice.)*: And do you despair, my sons, because Isaiah is dead? I will get you the word of another, another prophet in Israel, a man who has foreseen not only our present but our future: who sees, as in a dream, our sufferings, our torture, our final triumph—*(He opens his worn, old coat carefully and extracts a treasured volume.)* This is the Book of Daniel, inspired by the Lord and animated by the spirit of prophecy. Herein doth the wise man rejoice and foresee the triumph of Israel.

SIMON *(Reaching out his hand for it eagerly.)*: Would you entrust it to me, father? If we could only read it to our people, perhaps on a night before we go to battle, I am sure it will lead us to victory.

ELEAZAR *(Gloomily.)*: Alas! Yes, I fear Israel has fallen on evil times.

MATTATHIAS: My sons, my sons! You must not speak like this. The God of Israel fainteth not, nor is He weary.

JUDAS *(Charlie) (Rushing in elated)*: Courage! Hope, my brothers—praised be the God of Israel!

MATTATHIAS *(Embracing him.)*: Judas, my son—the leader of his people. My children, you bear witness that this day I call Judas the leader of his people.

JUDAS *(Bowing his head.)*: Father, I thank you!

MATTATHIAS: Judas, in your veins flows the blood of many centuries of warriors. Your brain is filled with fervor, your heart with faith. You alone can lead Israel to victory, and the tramp of the tyrant will go out of the land forever!

JONATHAN *(A bit protestingly.)*: But, father, is not Simon our oldest brother?

MATTATHIAS: True, Simon is my first-born, and he has the soul of the wise man. Simon shall be your guide, your adviser, your councillor; Judas, your military leader.

JUDAS: But you, father, you will be with us many years to lead and guide us.

MATTATHIAS *(Sinking exhausted on a chair.)*: My children, I hear often the voice of the spirit. I fear it will not now be many months before

I leave you. Judas, Simon, and the Book of Daniel must sweep you on to victory.

JUDAS *(His head high, his shoulders thrown back.)*: Victory! Listen, rumors gather in the marketplace. Menelaus, not content with waging war against his brothers, would now force them to accept the religion of the Greeks. If we do not accept their faith, we perish; already Antiochus has desecrated our altars and our ark. At the very entrance to their cave of refuge he slaughtered the Hasidim. Are we cowards that we, with red blood in our veins, should suffer this to continue? What is our life, our breath, our naked strength, if not for the conquest of our enemy? Should we want to live without our religion? the dear God of our fathers? I call upon you, my brothers— now is the time—today the very hour when we should give our breath and strength and hope to the conquest of the tyrant!

ALL *(With great fervor.)*: We trust you, Judas. You shall lead us to victory!

SIMON *(Holding up the book.)*: Judas and the Book of Daniel!

JUDAS *(Taking it eagerly.)*: The Book of Daniel—Just what my soldiers need—Long have they cried for a prophet in Israel—Long have they thirsted for an inspired word—With this I can strengthen their faith in the Almighty!

ALL *(Drawing their swords.)*: You lead, Judas, we follow!

MATTATHIAS: One word more! Beware, my sons, fight not in the open. Seek the hills and the secret hiding places. Remember that you are few, though stout of heart; they are many and powerful.

JUDAS *(Still inspired.)*: Yes, many and powerful! But, father, the good God must watch over us, for our secret places are discovered, our caves and hiding places watched. From now on we must fight in the open. A few leagues away the Judeans await us—await our coming. Armed with a greater faith than we have ever had, they must follow us into the very stronghold of the enemy. The Book of Daniel will light our way, and the good God of Israel deliver our enemy into our hands.

ALL: You lead! We follow!

(All rush out with great enthusiasm.)

MATTATHIAS *(Left alone with bowed head.)*: My sons, I pray for you!

PHILIP *(After a few moments' silence.)*: Oh, but that was wonderful! Charlie, it must be great to be Judas. I only wish that mamma would let me have a try.

CHARLIE: You really liked it? Honest? I think I was pretty good myself.

PHILIP *(Eagerly.)*: Liked it! Will you let me shake your hand?

(Charlie shakes his hand sheepishly.)

HARRY: But, Phil, we've got another scene. You wait for that. I believe it's the grandest of all.

SAMMY: Here's where old Antiochus "gets his." Got another chair for me to lie down on?

PHILIP *(Eagerly.)*: Take the sofa—O, please, hurry, hurry.

(They all push the sofa, stage center. Sammy lies down on it, Harry and Charlie wait a little to the rear. The rest group themselves about Philip, listening eagerly.)

ANTIOCHUS *(Lying on the sofa and groaning.)*: And I am left alone to die! Egypt is in ruins, and Persia desolate. Gone is my pomp, my power, my glory! My mercenaries desert me, my courtiers forget me. All Israel mocks me. They jeer at me, and rejoice in my defeat. *(Almost in delirium.)* Menelaus, the traitor, for whom I have done everything, even he deserts me in the hour of my need.

MENELAUS *(Enters hurriedly, holding his arm as if wounded.)*: Alas, your Majesty! I have no good news. The God of Israel is triumphant!

ANTIOCHUS *(Resting on his elbow.)*: Wait, you dog of a Jew! You to whom I have given power and wealth unlimited, have you too failed?

MENELAUS *(With head bowed.)*: Judas is a mighty force, he pursues me like death. Wherever I go, there he is before me. He is armed with the power of the Lord; I cannot resist his onslaughts.

ANTIOCHUS: But did you not destroy their temple, spread the blood of swine upon their altars? What force can they have left? What is this Book of Daniel?

MENELAUS *(Snarling with rage.)*: Alas! It comes from Mattathias, the father of the Hasmoneans. With Judas to lead them and the Book to give them faith, the Jews are invincible.

ANTIOCHUS: Bah! The Jews! The Jews! Can I never get rid of them, wipe them out forever? My armies advance against them, my mercenaries slaughter them, and still the God of Israel lives, bah!

MENELAUS *(Bowing his head in despair.)*: Yes, the God of Israel lives!

(Simon steps forward quickly with the transparent fire-screen, which makes an improvised veil, behind which Judas takes his station, and begins to speak in a low, sepulchral voice. At first Antiochus does not seem to hear. Then, half-frightened, he turns on his elbow, but being crazed and half-delirious, he pictures Judas as the voice of conscience, which in reality he is. To the dying man the voice is but a figment of the brain.)

JUDAS: The God of Israel lives—

ANTIOCHUS: The voice of Judas? the voice of Judas—

(He crouches in fear, and Menelaus cowers at the foot of the couch, he too fearing to look up.)

JUDAS *(Continuing as if he had not heard.)*: The God of Israel lives and watches over all his children—watches and guards them well. You, Menelaus, the traitor, and you, Antiochus, the tyrant, will be food for the worms and rotting under the ground many, many years, while the God of Israel and His children will continue down into the centuries—

(As Judas holds his sword aloft, and Antiochus and Menelaus crouch in agony, Aunt Bella, Doctor Slesinger, and Mrs. Beckman stand watching in the doorway, the last restrained with difficulty by the doctor. Molly stumbles into the opposite door, rubbing her eyes sleepily. The boys do not notice them, but as Judas is about to continue, Philip rushes over to him and grasps his arm excitedly.)

PHILIP: O, Judas, you're just wonderful. I want to be a warrior too—and fight old Antiochus—Please, please, won't you let me help to fight for Israel?

CHARLIE *(Turning shamefacedly and seeing Miss Bella in the doorway.)*: Is it all right, Miss Bella? May Phil help too?

BELLA *(Hurrying over.)*: Does he *want* to fight for Israel?

MRS. BECKMAN *(Hurrying over.)*: My poor darling! I'm sure all this has been too much for you.

PHILIP *(Pushing her away excitedly.)*: But, mamma, I'm not sick. I only want to be a soldier and fight the old Greeks—another Judas, mamma.

DOCTOR SLESINGER *(To Aunt Bella.)*: Even Mrs. Beckman must see how successful your prescription is.

CHARLIE *(Anxiously, as Miss Bella pats his head.)*: I did Judas just as well as ever I could.

PHILIP: Oh, and I do so want to help him, if you'll only let me be a Has-mo-ne-an.

BELLA: Ask your mother, Philip.

MRS. BECKMAN *(Hesitating, then looking around at the eager faces of the little boys and the glowing face of little Philip, as she nods assent.)*: Another—little—Judas.

(The boys all crowd around, eagerly welcoming Philip.)

Curtain.

THE HANUKKAH LIGHT

MY TOPCOAT WAS ALREADY IN my hand, and yet I could not decide: to go, or not to go—to give my lesson! O, it is so unpleasant outside, such horrible weather!—A mile's trudge—and then what?

"Once more: pakád, pakádti"—once more: the old housemaster, who has got through his sixty and odd years of life without knowing any grammar; who has been ten times to Leipzig, two or three times to Dantzig; who once all but landed in Constantinople—and who cannot understand such waste of money: Grammar, indeed? A fine bargain!

Then the young housemaster, who allows that it is far more practical to wear earlocks, a fur cap, and a braided kaftan, to consult with a "good Jew," and not to know any grammar...not that he is otherwise than orthodox himself...but he is obliged, as a merchant, to mix with men, to wear a hat and a stiff shirt; to permit his wife to visit the theatre; his daughter, to read books; and to engage a tutor for his son....

"My father, of course, knows best! But one must move with the times!" He cannot make up his mind to be left in the lurch by the times! "I only beg of you," he said to me, "don't make an unbeliever of the boy! I will give you," he said, "as much as would pay for a whole lot of grammar, if you will *not* teach him that the earth goes round the sun!"

And I promised that he should never hear it from, me, because— because this was my only lesson, and I had a sick mother at home!

To go, or not to go?

The whole family will be present to watch me when I give my lesson. She also?

She sits in the background, always deep in a book; now and again she lifts her long, silken lashes, and a little brightness is diffused through the room; but so seldom, so seldom!

And what is to come of it?

Nothing ever *can* come of it, except heartache.

"Listen!" My mother's weak voice from the bed recalls me to myself. "The Feldscher says, if only I had a pair of warm, woollen socks, I might creep about the room a little!"

That, of course, decides it.

Except for the lady of the house, who has gone to the play, as usual without the knowledge of her father-in-law, I find the whole family assembled round the pinchbeck samovar. The young housemaster acknowledges my greeting with a negligent "a good year to you!" and goes on turning over in his palm a pack of playing cards. Doubtless he expects company.

The old housemaster, in a peaked cap and a voluminous Turkish Dressing gown, does not consider it worthwhile to remove from his lips the long pipe with its amber mouthpiece, or to lift his eyes from off his well-worn book of devotions. He merely gives me a nod, and once more sinks his attention in the portion appointed for Hanukkah.

She also is intent on her reading, only her book, as usual, is a novel.

My arrival makes a disagreeable impression on my pupil.

"O, I say!" and he springs up from his seat at the table, and lowers his black-ringed, little head defiantly, "lessons today?"

"Why not?" smiles his father.

"But it's Hanukkah!" answers the boy, tapping the floor with his foot, and pointing to the first light, which has been placed in the window, behind the curtain, and fastened to a bit of wood.

"Quite right!" growls the old gentleman.

"Well, well," says the younger one, with indifference, "you must excuse him for once!"

I have an idea that *she* has become suddenly paler, that she bends lower over her book.

I wish them all good night, but the young housemaster will not let me go.

"You must stay to tea!"

"And to 'rascals with poppy-seed!'" cries my pupil, joyfully. He is quite willing to be friends, so long as there is no question of "pakád, pakádti."

I am diffident as to accepting, but the boy seizes my hand, and, with a roguish smile on his restless features, he places a chair for me opposite to his sister's.

Has he observed anything? On *my* side, of course, I mean....

She is always abstracted and lost in her reading. Very likely she looks upon me as an idler, or even worse...she does not know that I have a sick mother at home!

"It will soon be time for you to dress!" exclaims her father, impatiently.

"Soon, very soon, Tatishe!" she answers hastily, and her pale cheeks take a tinge of color.

The young housemaster abandons himself once more to his reflections; my pupil sends a top spinning across the table; the old man lays down his book, and stretches out a hand for his tea.

Involuntarily I glance at the Hanukkah light opposite to me in the window.

It burns so sadly, so low, as if ashamed in the presence of the great, silvered lamp hanging over the dining table, and lighting so brilliantly the elegant tea service.

I feel more depressed than ever, and do not observe that she is offering me a glass of tea.

"With lemon?" her melancholy voice rouses me.

"Perhaps you prefer milk?" says her father.

"Look out! The milk is smoked!" cries my pupil, warningly.

An exclamation escapes her:

"How can you be so…!"

Silence once more. Nothing but a sound of sipping and a clink of spoons. Suddenly my pupil is moved to inquire:

"After all, teacher, what *is* Hanukkah?"

"Ask the rabbi tomorrow in school!" says the old man, impatiently.

"Eh!" is the prompt reply, "I should think a tutor knew better than a rabbi!"

The old man casts an angry glance at his son, as if to say: "Do you see?"

"*I* want to know about Hanukkah, too!" she exclaims softly.

"Well, well," says the young housemaster to me, "let us hear your version of Hanukkah by all means!"

"It happened," I begin, "in the days when the Greeks oppressed us in the land of Israel. The Greeks—" But the old man interrupts me with a sour look:

"In the Benedictions it says: 'The wicked Kingdom of Javan.'"

"It comes to the same thing," observes his son, "what *we* call Javan, *they* call Greeks."

"The Greeks," I resume, "oppressed us terribly! It was our darkest hour. As a nation, we were threatened with extinction. After a few ill-starred risings, the life seemed to be crushed out of us, the last gleam of hope had faded. Although in our own country, we were trodden under foot like worms."

The young housemaster has long ceased to pay me any attention. His ear is turned to the door; he is intent on listening for the arrival of a guest.

But the old housemaster fixes me with his eye, and, when I have a second time used the word "oppressed," he can no longer contain himself:

"A man should be explicit! 'Oppressed'—what does that convey to me? They forced us to break the Sabbath; they forbade us to keep our festivals, to study the Law, even to practice circumcision."

"You play 'Preference'?" inquires the younger gentleman, suddenly, "or perhaps even poker?"

Once more there is silence, and I continue: "The misfortune was aggravated by the fact that the nobility and the wealthy began to feel ashamed of their own people, and to adopt Greek ways of living. They used to frequent the gymnasiums."

She and the old gentleman look at me in astonishment.

"In the gymnasiums of those days," I hasten to add, "there was no studying—they used to practice gymnastics, naked, men and women together—"

The two pairs of eyes lower their gaze, but the young housemaster raises his with a flash.

"*What* did you say?"

I make no reply, but go on to speak of the theatres where men fought wild beasts and oxen, and of other Greek manners and customs which must have been contrary to Jewish tradition.

"The Greeks thought nothing of all this; they were bent on effacing every trace of independent national existence. They set up an altar in the street with an 'Avodeh zoroh,' and commanded us to sacrifice to it."

"What is that?" she asks in Polish.

I explain; and the old man adds excitedly:

"And a swine, too! We were to sacrifice a swine to it!"

"And there was found a Jew to approach the altar with an offering.

"But that same day, the old Maccabeus, with his five sons, had come down from the hills, and before the Greek soldiers could intervene, the miserable apostate was lying in his blood, and the altar was torn down. In one second the rebellion was ablaze. The Maccabees, with a handful of men, drove out the far more numerous Greek garrisons. The people were set free!

"It is that victory we celebrate with our poor, little illumination, with our Hanukkah lights."

"What?" and the old man, trembling with rage, springs out of his chair. "*That* is the Hanukkah light? Come here, wretched boy!" he screams to his grandson, who, instead of obeying, shrinks from him in terror.

The old man brings his fist down on the table, so that the glasses ring again.

"It means—when we had driven out the unclean sons of Javan, there was only one little cruse of holy olive oil left...."

But a fit of coughing stops his breath, and his son hastens up, and assists him into the next room.

I wish to leave, but she detains me.

"You are against assimilation, then?" she asks.

"To assimilate," I reply, "is to consume, to eat, to digest. We assimilate beef and bread, and others wish to assimilate us—to eat us up like bread and meat."

She is silent for a few seconds, and then she asks anxiously:

"But will there always, always be wars and dissensions between the nations?"

"O no!" I answer, "one point they must all agree—in the end."

"And that is?"

"Humanity. When each is free to follow his own bent, then they will all agree."

She is lost in thought, she has more to say, but there comes a tap at the door—

"Mamma!" she exclaims under her breath, and escapes, after giving me her hand—for the first time!

On the next day but one, while I was still in bed, I received a letter by the postman.

The envelope bore the name of her father's firm: "Jacob Berenholz."

My heartbeat like a sledgehammer. Inside there were only ten rubles—my pay for the month that was not yet complete.

Goodbye, lesson!

The Enemies of Israel:
A Hanukkah Fantasy in One Act

MR.SOLOMON

MRS. SOLOMON

JUDAH, their son, aged 13

SIMEON, their son, aged 12

MIRIAM, their daughter, aged 10

HANNAH, their niece, aged 9, a visitor from a distant town

MARY, their maid

IGNORANCE

GREED

FEAR

EVIL

TRUTH

12 HANDMAIDENS OF TRUTH

12 CHILDREN, guests at party in Scene II

PROLOGUE

Dear friends, who've come to see our little play,
We bid you greeting. For your presence here
We thank you, and with all our hearts we pray
You will enjoy our playlet. Have no fear.
We'll do our best to tell the season's story.
Give heed, I pray, and hear of Israel's glory.

SCENE I

The parlor of the Solomon home. It is a modern room, well furnished, cozy and comfortable. There is a door, rear, leading to the hall and an open doorway, right, leading to the dining room. In the right front wall is a fireplace. On left side of room is a table. On the other side is a large armchair before the fire. At rise of curtain, Simeon is at table reading and two girls are on the armchair before the fire.

(Enter Judah, door R., chewing.)

SIMEON: Where've you been, Judah? *(Sees him chewing.)* Eating again? Out in the kitchen, eh?

JUDAH *(With a smile.)*: Yes, I was out helping Mary prepare dinner. You know she is so busy at holiday time, I like to do what little I can for her.

MIRIAM: I can imagine how you helped her. I guess you were showing her how to get rid of her cakes.

SIMEON: Yes, Judah's pretty good at the disappearing act. I suppose when he grows up he'll join a circus and become a sword swallower.

JUDAH: You needn't talk, Simeon, I saw you eat three cakes at Hannah's party the other night.

MIRIAM: And two portions of ice cream.

HANNAH: And two bananas.

SIMEON: Stop, stop, that's enough. I guess none of us like to fast. Did you see anything good out in the kitchen, Judah?

JUDAH: There's all kinds of goodies. Mother certainly does get up things in great shape when Hanukkah comes. By the way, Hannah, this will be your first Hanukkah in the big city, won't it?

HANNAH: It will, and I'm glad to be here. Auntie told me of your beautiful service and I'm so anxious to hear it. I wish it were six o'clock.

JUDAH: It's just five now. You'll have to wait a bit. We can't have dinner until father gets home from the office.

MIRIAM: I wonder where mother is. I wish she would tell us about Hanukkah. I love to hear about it.

(Enter Mrs. Solomon, door, center.)

MRS. S: Hello, children. I've been looking for you. Are you all ready for Hanukkah? *(The girls rush to her.)*

SIMEON: Yes, mother, we are all ready. The candles are ready, *(Pointing to a candelabrum on the table.)* and Judah's tasted all the food—and we're all anxious to hear the service, especially Hannah, who has never heard it before.

MRS. S: Haven't you, Hannah?

HANNAH: No, auntie, dear. In our little town there are no other Jewish families and sometimes, at the holidays, father doesn't read the service. Last time he read the Hanukkah service I was too little to understand. And I'm so anxious to know all about it. Won't you tell us about it now, auntie, dear?

ALL: Yes, do, mother.

MRS. S *(Going to armchair and sitting down; girls sit on floor on each side of her.)*: My dears, I'll be glad to tell you the story of Hanukkah. But you must promise not to tell father when he comes. He'll be surprised to find you know all about it.

JUDAH: Won't he be pleased? And perhaps, if he's very, very pleased, he'll—he'll—well, perhaps he'll give us all an extra piece of cake.

SIMEON: Judah, be still, stop talking about eating for a while. Mother wants to tell us about Hanukkah. *(All listen closely.)*

MRS. S: Once upon a time—

JUDAH: Oh, it's a fairy tale.

MRS. S: Better than a fairy tale, because it's all true. Once upon a time, many hundreds of years ago, the Jews lived in a distant land called Palestine.

MIRIAM: Is it far away, mother?

MRS. S: Yes, my dear, it is very far.

HANNAH: Farther than—than New York?

MRS. S: Yes, dear, much farther. It was far across the ocean on the other side of the world; where the great desert ends and meets the land of beautiful flowers and luscious fruits.

SIMEON: Wait one minute, mother, I'll find it in the Atlas. Then perhaps Miriam and Hannah will enjoy your story more. *(He reaches down on the table and takes out an Atlas. He opens it and searches for the page.)* P-Pa-Pal-Pale-Palestine. Here it is. *(Pointing with his finger. The children all rush to see it.)*

MIRIAM: Yes, yes, and here's the Red Sea where Moses crossed with the people of Israel.

JUDAH: And here's Jerusalem, where King Solomon built the Temple. And here's—what's this, mother, M-o-d-i-n?

MRS. S *(Looking over children's shoulders.)*: That's Modin. Modin—that's the scene of our Hanukkah story, Judah. I'm glad you found it. *(Judah swells with pride.)*

SIMEON *(Laughingly.)*: Christofo Colombo number two.

MRS. S: Now, children, to continue. *(She reseats herself in the armchair and all listen closely.)* Here in this beautiful land lived the children of Israel. Surrounded by enemies who prayed to idols, they remained true to the one and only God; and morning and evening their songs of prayer and praise rose over the vine-covered hillsides of Palestine. But evil days came upon the children of God. A powerful enemy, the Syrians, conquered their country. Under the leadership of their king, Antiochus Epiphanes, they strove to make the people of Israel forsake God. Hannah. Antiochus Epiphanes, what a horrible name! Mrs. S. And a horrible king he was. He had Grecian idols of stone put into the Temple and he ordered the Jews to pray to them. All who refused were to be killed.

HANNAH: Or, dear, I'm glad I didn't live in those days. Did any Jews pray to idols?

MRS. S: Yes, I'm sorry to say, some did. But most of them remained true to their God, and many were killed for so doing. But they died a noble death.

JUDAH: And how about my Modin? What happened there?

MRS. S: You are all puffed up about your Modin, aren't you, Judah? You have a right to be. In this little town lived an old priest, named Mattathias, with his five sons, Judah, John, Eliezer, Jonathan and Simeon.

SIMEON: Simeon, that's me.

JUDAH: Be still. How could you have lived so long ago? And besides, father's name is Philip, not Mata—Mata—*(Struggling.)*

MRS. S: Mattathias, dear. This old priest was a man of great courage. When the king's men came to put the Syrian idols in the Temple, one of the Jews, who had no courage whatever, fell on his knees before the idol and bowed to it. Enraged at this desertion of the true God, Mattathias struck at the cowardly Jew with his sword, and slew him. Then crying out to his sons, "Follow me!" he cut his way out to the countryside where he stirred up his people to revolt against the tyrant.

JUDAH: And—then—I'll bet they had a war!

MRS. S: Yes, and what a war it was! For a long time the people had hoped for a leader and at last one had come. With shouts of praise they joined Mattathias' band and left their homes. to fight for their faith and freedom. When the old priest died he turned over his command to Judah.

JUDAH: Judah! That's me!

SIMEON: Why didn't he give it to Simeon?

MRS. S: Judah was the third of the five sons, but he was the noblest and the bravest, and the old man knew he would grow up to be a great leader. If you only grow to be like him, Judah, I will have no cause to fear for you.

JUDAH *(With great gusto.)*: Show me the Syrians! *(All laugh.)*

MRS. S: Mattathias' family came to be known as the Maccabees and the war they waged, the Maccabean war. For years they fought. Often they were defeated, but they had faith in God. After three years of bitter fighting Judah fought his way with his troops into Jerusalem. There in the newly-cleansed Temple the perpetual lamp was gladly and solemnly lighted. Eight days of feasting and of prayer were declared, and thus was celebrated the first Hanukkah. Now every year we burn our festive lights for eight days in memory of those brave Jews who were not afraid to die for their faith and who rescued it from those that wished to destroy it. But though Judah had recaptured Jerusalem the Syrians still held other portions of Palestine in their grasp. The brave Maccabees were determined not to give up the struggle until the whole of Palestine was freed of the invader. The brave Judah fell in battle, but his brother Simeon took up the task. Year after year the Jews fought on. Step by step their land was wrested from the oppressor, until at last, after twenty-seven years of bitter fighting, the Syrians were completely defeated. The army of Antiochus was crushed and fled. Palestine was once more free of the invader and the religion of Israel was saved from destruction. That is all, my dears. It is a simple story, but in all your books you will find none more beautiful, or more stirring.

(All sit in silent rapture.)

HANNAH: Isn't it wonderful? Isn't it beautiful? It makes me real proud to be a Jewess.

JUDAH: It's certainly great. I wish I lived in those days. I'd like to fight some enemies. Gee, Simeon, why haven't we got some enemies to fight? All we can do is have snow fights in winter and Indian fights in summer, and if I get into a fight with Mickey Jones, I get whipped for it when I get home.

MRS. S: And so you should.

SIMEON: But the Jews haven't any enemies now, have they, mother? That is, real enemies. The soldiers never come to bother us; the policemen don't say anything to us, except when we play ball on the front street. Sometimes the boys call us names, but names don't hurt; and besides, I know they don't know what they are saying, so I don't mind much. But we've no real enemies.

MRS. S: Ah, my boys, we have lots of enemies to fight.

JUDAH and SIMEON *(Breathlessly.)*: Who are they?

MIRIAM: It can't be the Syrians, 'cause there aren't any 'round here.

SIMEON: It can't be the Irish, 'cause they're so much fun. Mary wouldn't hurt a cat.

HANNAH: And it can't be the Germans, 'cause old Schmidt that runs the candy store is as kind as he can be. He always gives us an extra piece.

JUDAH: I know, I'll bet it's the Rooshians.

MRS. S *(With a sigh.)*: You're partly right there, Judah. There in the East our brethren still die by the thousands. But our worst enemies are here, in our own country, in our own city.

JUDAH: Who are they? *(Doubling his fist ferociously.)* Where are they? I'll get up an army like Judah Maccabee.

(Simeon salutes him.)

MRS. S: Think hard, my dears, you will find out. When father comes home from town I'll tell him to ask you and the one who guesses will get a surprise.

JUDAH: Some cake, eh?

MRS. S: Better than that, my little hungry man. Come now, girls, Judah's getting too warlike; we'd better go. Come upstairs with me. Father will soon be home. *(Exit Mrs. S. and girls, door center.)*

SIMEON: Who can our enemies be, Judah?

JUDAH: I don't know, Sim. But I'm going to find out. *(He sits down in armchair with his head in his hands.)*

SIMEON *(Goes to door, right.)*: I'm going out to the kitchen, Jud. Maybe I'll find the enemy there.

JUDAH *(Looking up.)*: You won't.

SIMEON: Why?

JUDAH: You won't have time.

SIMEON: Why not?

JUDAH: You'll be too busy looking for cake.

SIMEON: Well, people who live in glass houses—

JUDAH: Shouldn't look for cake. *(As Simeon goes.)* Ho, Sim! *(Simeon reappears.)* To save time, I'll tell you. It's in the upper drawer of the cupboard. *(Laughs lightly. Simeon runs out door, right. Simeon runs back as though trying to escape someone; exit by door, center. Mary rushes in after him, rolling pin in hand.)*

MARY: Shure, and that's where they'll stay! Don't yez be gettin' in that cupboard again. *(Exit, door, right.)*

JUDAH: I wonder who those enemies are. It's not the Irish, nor the Germans, nor the Americans—no, we're all Americans. *(He yawns and slides down into a reclining posture.)* Who are our enemies? *(He grows very quiet; stage has been growing darker; he falls asleep; stage grows darker; curtain falls slowly.)*

Scene II

Our first short scene is done, dear friends.
And you have heard how God his victories doth win.
How Syrian king and heathen idols, too.
Were beaten by the enemies of sin.
How Judah and his Maccabeans brave,
Fought on for many years against the foe.
Their country and their glorious faith to save.
That God and living Truth the world might know.
And now as Judah of our story sleeps.
Come with us to the Land of Dreams, and see
How there, while tossing in his slumber deep.
He found who now are Israel's enemies.
Forget our humble tale—a journey take
Upon a silver-footed sunshine beam;
There where none doth ever come awake
We both shall see our sleeping Judah's dream.

THE DREAM

The curtain rises upon the same scene as Scene I. The room is arranged for a party of about twelve boys and girls. Guests are present. Judah, Simeon, Miriam, Hannah and Mrs. Solomon are also in the room. Judah is of course no longer in the arm-chair. There is general merriment as at a party.

JUDAH *(Excitedly.)*: Wasn't the service great? Three cheers for Judah Maccabee.

ALL: Ray, ray, for Judah Maccabee!

SIMEON: Let's play Syrians again.

ALL: Yes, yes, let's play Syrians.

(The group divides: six boys and girls on one side, six on the other side, front stage. Judah heads group to left who are the Jews, and Simeon heads group to right who are the Syrians. Mr. and Mrs. S. are in the rear, watching. The following is sung to an old playground melody with a martial air. The groups advance alternately toward the center of stage as though charging an enemy and then retire to original position, then other side advances and retires, and so on to end. The entire game rnust be given a very martial air by the drill execution and the body carriage of the actors.)

(Simeon's side advancing.)
                    Tell us, have you any God?
(Retire.)   We are the Syrians.
(Advance.)   Tell us, have you any God?
(Retire.)   We're the Syrian soldiers!
(Judah's side advancing.)
                    Yes, we have but one true God.
(Retire.)   We all are Israel.
(Advance.)   Yes, we have but one true God.
(Retire.)   We are Israel's soldiers!
(Simeon's side.)
(Advance.)   Now, our kind Antiochus,
                    King of the Syrians,
                    Says you must bow down to us.
                    We're the Syrian soldiers.

(Judah's side.)
(Advance.)   We will ne'er bow down to you;
                    We're God's own soldiers—
                    For our hearts to Him are true.
                    We're the Jewish soldiers.

(Simeon's side.)
                    You must pray to idols fine.
                    We are the Syrians.
                    Eat their meat and drink their wine.
                    We are the Syrians.
                    Bow yourselves and slaughter swine.
                    We're the Syrian soldiers!

(Judah's side.)

> To your God we ne'er will pray.
> We all are Israel!
> Neither shall we run away.
> We all are Israel!
> We will fight, to God we'll pray,
> For we are Israel's soldiers!

(Simeon's side.)

> Run, you Hebrews. Run, run, run,
> We are the Syrians.
> We will slay you, every one.
> For we're the Syrian soldiers!

(Judah's side.)

> Strike, O Jews, for Israel's God.
> We fight for Israel!
> We are His own lightning rod.
> We're Israel's soldiers!

(Simeon's side.)
(Retire.)

> Run, O Syrians, let us fly.
> Come, run, O Syrians!
> Let us run or we shall die.
> Come, let's flee, O Syrians!

(Judah's side.)

> We have conquered by God's aid.
> We all are Israel.
> We have fought and we have prayed.
> We're Israel's soldiers.
> Now the Syrians we have flayed,
> For we are Israel's soldiers.

(All laugh, break ranks and clap hands; general merriment.)

MARY *(Going out door, right.)*: Wurra—Wurran, they'd beat the Irish.

JUDAH: We sure did lick 'em. Just like Judah of old and his Maccabees. Say, what's this coming? Look! *(He points to the audience. All children rush forward and look intently. Hold position. Down aisle comes a figure in a black robe and black tights. His head is built up like a box. Only his face shows. On his arm he carries a big book. On his back is a sign in large letters, "Ignorance.")*

JUDAH: Look, what is it? *(Ignorance walks up steps leading: to stage and stands poised for a minute. At top, children run to back of stage in fear. Mr. Solomon comes up to him from left. Ignorance turns to face Mr. Solomon, center, stage.)*

MR. S *(In authoritative tone.)*: Who are you?

IGNORANCE *(In a dull monotone which he maintains throughout.)*: I dunno.

MR. S: Where do you come from?

IGNORANCE: I dunno.

MR.S: What do you want?

IGNORANCE: I dunno.

JUDAH *(Mockingly.)*: I dunno. I dunno. What do you know?

IGNORANCE *(After a pause.)*: I dunno. *(All in despair.)*

MR. S: See here, my good friend, what do you mean by coming here unasked? Give an account of yourself. Where do you come from? What are you doing here?

IGNORANCE: I dunno. I just walked in.

MRS. S: A Daniel come to judgment.

JUDAH: Why didn't you come in through the door?

IGNORANCE: Is there a door?

HANNAH: Did you ever in your life hear of anyone so stupid?

IGNORANCE: Stupid? That's my cousin.

Mr. S: Well, who are you?

Ignorance: My name's here. *(Pointing to his back.)*

All: Why, his name is Ignorance.

Ignorance: Yes, yes, that's it.

Mr. S: Well, if you can't read, why on earth do you carry that book?

Ignorance: I found it there when I was born.

Judah *(Who has been examining book.)*: Why, it's all covered with dust. It looks as if it has never been opened.

Ignorance: No, I never opened it. I didn't know it could open.

A little girl from rear: Boo hoo, boo hoo, etc. *(Bursting into tears.)*

Mrs. S *(Rushing to her side.)*: What's wrong, dear?

Girl *(Crying all the while.)*: I know him. He is Ignorance. Boo hoo, now I know what mother meant. *(Crying.)*

Mrs. S: When, dear?

Girl: Yesterday I wouldn't study and mother said I'd grow up to be ignorant, and he's Ignorance, and I don't wanna be like him. Boo hoo. *(Etc.)*

Mrs. S: Then you must study, my dear, and you won't be like him. The horrid thing.

Judah *(Excitedly.)*: Look, look, who's this? Who's this?

(All look. Down aisle and up steps comes a second figure. He is a fat-bellied being with a red face and an evil grin. On his arm he holds a large sack filled with metals, with a large dollar sign on it. He jingles it up and down as he walks. Occasionally he stops, as though

picking up coins, which he throws into bag. On his back is a large sign, "Greed." The children retire to rear again. Greed comes up to stage in like manner as Ignorance. He wears a yellow robe and green tights.)

GREED: Hello, folks; hello. Ignorance. Been here long?

IGNORANCE *(Turning to Mr. S.):* I dunno. Have I?

MR. S: No, thank heavens, he hasn't. *(To Ignorance.)* And who's this?

IGNORANCE: That's my brother.

GREED: Yes. I'm Greed.

MR. S: Greed? What are you doing here?

GREED: I follow Ignorance. Wherever he goes, I follow. He just goes as he goes, but I get as I go.

MR. S: What do you get?

GREED: I get anything I can. I like dollars best. It seems to me you people don't know me. Out where I come from I'm somebody. I've got more money than anybody for miles around. *(Proudly.)* I've got two houses full of silver and gold things, with beautiful, expensive furniture—imported, all of it. And I've got two automobiles and four servants. I'm a respected citizen, I am. I'm a pillar in the church. Why, do you know, I've got the biggest house, the largest automobile, and the finest country house in the world? Haven't I, brother? *(Turning to Ignorance.)*

IGNORANCE: I dunno.

GREED: I might have known you wouldn't know, old block. Say, what's that? *(Seeing silver ornament on table and going over to it.)* That's pretty, isn't it? Not so pretty as the one I have at home, but I like it first rate. Guess I'll take it along, *(Reaches for it.)*

Mr. S *(Rushing to him and grasping it from his hand.)*: See here, you Greed, or whoever you are, let that be. How dare you touch that? I suppose you'll want the house and everything that's in it, next.

Greed *(Withdrawing his hand.)*: Well, I might just decide to take a few things. If I do, I'll take it. Anything I see, I want, and anything I want, I get. *(The children are in fear.)*

A little boy *(Bursting into tears.)*: Boo hoo, I'll never do it again. I'll never do it again.

Mrs. S *(Rushing to him.)*: What's wrong, dear?

Boy *(Between sobs.)*: Yesterday I ate up all the candy in sister's box and mother said I was a very greedy boy—an'—an' he's Greedy—an'—an', Boo hoo, I don't wanna be like him. Boo hoo.

Judah *(In a loud voice, to Greed.)*: Just you dare to take anything here. Just you dare.

Simeon *(Excitedly.)*: Look, look, who's this? Another one. Look! *(All rush forward and look. A third figure comes down the aisle. He is thin, dressed in a black robe and black tights, with a large yellow streak down his back. As the others have done, he comes up to stage.)*

Greed: Well, Fear, what are you after?

Fear *(Timidly.)*: You know I always come after you, Greed. I heard these people quarrelling with you and I knew my place was near your heart. Greed, I would have been here sooner, but I couldn't.

Greed: Why not?

Fear: I was afraid, so I ran away, and I grew tired and had to lie down to rest. I lay down in a boy's heart and it was so cozy there I hated to leave. But I'll go back there again.

Mrs. S: Who is this Fear? What are you doing here? *(To Mr. S.)* He will enter the children's hearts. Let us drive them away.

A LITTLE GIRL *(Crying.)*: Boo hoo, it was all his fault. It was his fault. *(Pointing to Fear.)*

MRS. S *(Rushing to her.)*: Don't cry, dear. What is it?

GIRL: Boo hoo, it's all his fault. Last night I wouldn't go to bed in the dark. I made mother sit beside my bed till I fell asleep. Boo hoo, she said I was a bad girl because I had so much fear of nothing, and he's Fear, and I don't want him any more. Boo hoo.

JUDAH *(Excitedly.)*: Look, father, look, here comes another!

(All look. Down aisle comes a fourth figure. He is roughly dressed, and dirty. On his back is a sign, "Evil." He comes up to stage as others have done. He is dressed in red robe and tights.)

MIRIAM: Isn't he horrible! *(The children are afraid.)*

EVIL *(In a rough voice.)*: Hello, my brothers., I knew I'd find you here.

MR. S *(In a loud voice.)*: See here, you, what are you doing here? Who are you and your vile companions?

EVIL: Don't you know, sir? Why, I'm Evil. *(Points to sign on back.)* Here's my name. I keep it there because some people don't know me when they see me. These are my brothers. Ignorance, there, always goes first. Wherever he goes, Greed follows. Then Fear comes along, and I'm last. Where you find Ignorance, you'll find Greed; and wherever you find Ignorance and Greed, you'll find Fear; and wherever you find Ignorance, Greed and Fear, you'll find Evil, that's me.

A LITTLE BOY: O-oh, I'll be good. O-oh, I was bad yesterday and mother said I'd grow up to be an evil man, an' he's Evil and I don't wanna be like him. O-o-oh, I'll be good. I'll be good.*(Crying loudly; Mrs. Solomon comforts him.)*

MR. S *(To Evil.)*: But why do you come here with your brothers in this strange fashion? Why don't you come through the door like all good respectable people?

EVIL *(Laughingly.)*: Ha, ha! We're not good nor respectable. Ha, ha! I should say not.

GREED: I am.

EVIL: No, you're not. Greed. You only think you are. You're just like the rest of us. *(To Mr. S.)* You see, sir, we couldn't come any other way. We came this way *(extending his hand to audience)* because we live out there.

ALL: Where?

EVIL: Out there, among the people. That's where we come from. From right out among the people.

MR. S: But how did you get there?

EVIL: Ha, ha! We've always been out there, since the world began. That's our home.

JUDAH *(Curiously.)*: Don't you live on any street?

EVIL: Ha, ha! What fun. We live on every street—that is, one of our four. We always stick pretty close together. You're apt to find us all in the same place. Some people chase us away, but some people like us. We do our best to please 'em. See here, brothers, let's please these people. Let's sing for 'em, eh? Come on.

(They line up to sing. In the following, the character referred to sings his lines, the other three joining in to sing the lines marked "Chorus" and all except the character pointed out join in singing the refrain. Ignorance sings first.)

IGNORANCE: Who I am, I do not know.
        Ignorance they call me, so it must be so.

CHORUS: It must be so.

IGNORANCE: I live in the bodies of folks, 'tis said,
             Whose brains rattle, rattle in their empty heads!

CHORUS: In their empty heads.

(The other three, pointing to Ignorance.)

REFRAIN: That is Ignorance standing there.
         He knows nothing and he does not care.
         If you don't study as good folks should,
         Your head will turn to a block of wood.

(Ignorance taps his block-head.)

CHORUS: To a block of wood.

GREED *(Sings.)*: I am the fellow that folks call Greed.
         I want everything that other folks need.

CHORUS: That other folks need.

GREED: I want everything I ever see.
         Ha, ha! Don't laugh! There are many like me.

CHORUS: There are many like me.

(The other three, pointing to Greed.)

REFRAIN: There stands Greed with his sack of gold.
         He takes as much as his sack can hold.
         He has enough for three or four.
         But Greed is always looking for more!

CHORUS: He is looking for more!

FEAR *(Sings.)*: Fear am I, and I slink along,
         I'm just behind you when you're doing wrong.

CHORUS: When you're doing wrong.

FEAR: I'm afraid of the dark, dark night.
            But oh, I'm afraid, I'm afraid of the light.

(The other three, pointing to Fear.)

REFRAIN: Look, oh look, there stand Fear.
                When you're doing wrong, he's always near.
                Here and there through the world he darts,
                And tries to creep into peoples hearts

CHORUS: Oh, he creeps into your heart.

EVIL *(Sings.)*: I am Evil, of course you know.
            I always follow where the others go.

CHORUS: Where the others go.

EVIL: I fill little girls and boys with fright,
            For with me, right's wrong and wrong is right!

CHORUS: Wrong is right.

(The other three, pointing to Evil.)

REFRAIN: That is Evil standing there.
                Pray don't wander into his lair!
                If he catches you, he'll hold you tight.
                And he'll never let you do a thing that's right.

CHORUS: You'll never do right.

ALL TOGETHER: We are the horrible vices, four.
                        We're not the only ones; there are many more!
                        We go around and children test.
                        And if you are weak, we do the rest.
                        So you'd better watch out, our warning heed:
                        Study, study hard, and have no Greed;
                        Teach your heart to have no Fear;
                        And never, never play where Evil's near.

For we will get you if we only can.
We like to stay near the heart of man.
Listen to your heart, you may hear us roar;
For we are the horrible, rip-roar-roarable.
Horrible, horrible vices four.

(The children all crouch in fear. Mary enters door, right, with tray in hand; looks at vices with a gasp of amazement; drops tray; throws her hands in air.)

MARY: Glory be to Heaven! *(Rushes out door, right.)*

JUDAH: I should say you are horrible. I don't see how anybody could like you.

EVIL: Lots of people like us. Ignorance, there, has lots of friends. He met them when they started to school, and they all quit. He is always true to them. Some of his friends think they are not like Ignorance, but they are, only they don't know it. Greed, as he has no doubt told you, gets as he goes, and he gets almost everything. Fear's specialty is getting into things. People's hearts, mostly. He likes it there. I just follow the other three, like water follows the river—just naturally, you know. When I get a place that I like, I usually stay a while. *(Looking around.)* It's nice here. I'd like to stay here. *(To others.)* What do you say?

IGNORANCE: I don't mind. I might find some new friends here.

GREED: I'd like to stay here. I see a lot of nice things I could get.

FEAR: I'd like to stay. I see a lot of nice hearts I'd like to creep into. I'll bet they're nice cozy hearts, too. Evil. Yes, yes, boys, we'll stay a while.

(Mr. and Mrs. S. are in great fear. Just then a voice rises from the audience, clear and bell-like.)

VOICE—TRUTH: You will not stay. You will not stay.

(The four vices crouch together. All are amazed. From out in the audience there rise the soft strains of sweet music. Down the aisle comes Truth, a tall, stately, beautiful girl, followed by twelve little girls dressed in white robes. Truth sings the following, all joining [the group] in chorus, as the whole group led by Truth walks slowly down the aisle and up to the stage where Truth in center, surrounded by the maidens, confronts the vices. Each little girl carries a red torch in her hand. As they march, they wave the torches [flashlights may be used to good advantage] to and fro, in tune to the music. Song of Truth.)

Since first the darkness rolled away
And glorious rose the sun to view;
Since God raised man from out the clay.
And first flowers shone 'neath the dew;
We have coursed o'er the world, in the wake of man;
We have followed him everywhere!
We have searched out his heart and have lifted the ban.
That the spirits of Evil placed there.
We have entered the darkness and brought there the light,
Dispersing the spirits that deaden man's heart.
The banner of God we flung into sight.
As the soul of man wakens and Evils depart.

We are all the helpers of God!
We are the bearers of light!
We call men from Evil and Vice,
For justice and virtue to fight!
Come, O ye sons of men,
The banner of God is unfurled;
Flee, O ye spirits of Evil,
Let Truth make bright the world.

Truth and Chorus:
Come, O ye sons of men,
The banner of God is unfurled;
Flee, O ye spirits of Evil,
Let Truth illume the world.

(By this time all are on stage. Repeat chorus, if necessary, to get proper grouping. The vices are crouching at the foot-lights. When all is silent, Truth speaks.)

TRUTH: You will not stay here, vices four. I have pursued you since the beginning of time, enemies of mankind, and at last I have found you. You shall work your harm no more.

THE VICES *(Whining.)*: Who are you?

TRUTH *(Majestically.)*: I am Truth. These are my hand-maidens. Education and Religion. Have no fear, my children, where we come these four can do no harm. *(The children are comforted.)* Now, Evil, take your brothers—Go! I command you. *(They start toward audience.)* Not that way. There, behind you, go. *(They do not move.)* I need help. Strong arms and true hearts must help me. *(Judah, Simeon and two others step forward.)*

JUDAH: I will help you. Truth.

SIMEON: And I, too.

3D Boy: And I.

4TH BOY: And I, too. Now, Evil, take your brothers—Go! *(The vices slink out door, center, followed by the boys. All hold their position for a moment; then boys reappear.)*

TRUTH: Which path did they take?

JUDAH: The lower one.

TRUTH: Good! That is the path that leads to the forest of Despair, in the land of Nowhere. Once you get in it you can never get out. They will never return.

MR. S: Tell us, O Truth, why did you not let them go that way. *(Pointing to the audience.)*

TRUTH: Because I sent them into the Past. The Past is behind us. There they shall remain. This *(pointing about the stage)* is the Present. They could not go that way *(pointing to the audience)*, because there lies the Future, and the Future belongs to me! *(Proudly.)*

(All gaze at her fixedly; hold position, and curtain drops.)

Scene III

PROLOGUE

The dream is done and from the land of sleep
Come back, come back with me on silver wings,
Where Judah wakens from his slumber deep.
From dreams he comes again to living things.
We've traveled far, o'er dreamlit field and lake.
Here's earth again. O Judah! Come, awake!

The curtain rises. Scene same as end of Scene I. Judah is sleeping in armchair. Enter Mr. and Mrs. Solomon and the three children from door, center. Mr. Solomon switches on lights. They creep up and look at the sleeping boy. Judah is seen struggling in his sleep. He moves his arms, mutters and suddenly awakens. He jumps to his feet and looks around in amazement.

JUDAH: W-why—why—where am I? Wh-wh-where is Truth?

SIMEON *(Coming forward with a low bow.)*: Here I am, fair sir.

(All laugh except Judah.)

JUDAH: Why, I've been asleep. It must have been a dream. Oh, mother *(Rushing to her.)*, I've found it. I know who our enemies are.

SIMEON and THE GIRLS: Who are they?

JUDAH: The enemies of Israel aren't anybody. They're just spirits, unseen things. Ignorance, Greed, Fear, and the Evil that follows after them. They live inside us, in our hearts, in our own people. Judah fought the Syrians. We must fight ourselves. Or, mother, mother, thank God for Hanukkah that makes us look for our enemies and stirs us on to conquer them.

MR. S: Yes, children, Judah has dreamed it rightly. We are our own worst enemies. *(To Judah.)* After dinner, you may tell us of your dream. Meanwhile, here's the gift mother promised you. All. What is it?

JUDAH *(Opening package.)*: It's a Bible.

MR. S: Yes, my boy, read it. Read it, all of you. You were looking for Truth, Judah, when you awoke. You will find it here. *(Touches Bible.)*

(There is a pause; then Mary appears in door, right.)

MARY: Faith, Mrs. Solomon, an' dinner be served; that is, what's lift of it.

MRS. S: What's left of it?

MARY: Yes, mum. It's thim boys, mum. I started to prepare it at thray o'clock a-eaten' of it iver since.

JUDAH *(In mock surprise.)*: Why, Simeon! I'm surprised at you!

SIMEON *(In mock surprise.)*: Oh, Judah! How could you?

MIRIAM *(Stepping forward.)*: I cannot tell a lie, father, they both did it. *(All laugh.)*

MR. S *(At candelabrum on table.)*: Before we go in let us light our lights. It is six o'clock.

(The children get behind the candelabrum. Each child lights two lights from the end towards the middle, thus: Miriam, 1 and 3; Hannah, 5 and 7; Judah, 8 and 6; Simeon, 4 and 2. Mr. and Mrs. Solomon at each side of the table, smiling.)

1 MIRIAM: In the name of Education that frees us from Ignorance, I light this first light.

2 SIMEON: In the name of the Strength that comes from Knowledge that enables us to resist Greed, I light this second light.

3 MIRIAM: In the name of Virtue that comes from Strength and frees from Evil, I light this third light.

4 SIMEON: In the name of the Courage, inspired by Virtue, that knows no Fear, I light this fourth light.

5 HANNAH: In the name of the Justice with which we will make straight the way, I light this fifth light.

6 JUDAH: In the name of the Mercy, that shall temper life as it shall temper Justice, I light this sixth light.

7 HANNAH: In the name of the Faith that is as sure as the stars that never fail, I light this seventh light.

8 JUDAH: In the name of the Spirit of God, which is the spirit of Judaism, builded on Faith, which inspired the Maccabees of old, who inspire us in turn with the spirit that never dies, I light this eighth light.

(Then all join in singing the Hanukkah hymn to the old traditional melody. As they sing the curtain slowly falls.)

SONG: To Thee, O Lord, we pledge our lives,
Thine enemies to fight.
The hosts of Israel stand arrayed
To battle for the right.
As Judah's band fought on for Thee,
So will we fight through all our days;
Till ev'ry evil is no more,
And all the world sings loud Thy praise.

PICTURES OF THE PAST:

A HANUKKAH PLAY

CAST OF CHARACTERS

GRANDMOTHER
MOTHER
ESTHER, about fourteen years old
DAVID, about twelve years old
HELEN, about nine years old
LEO, about six years old

SCENE—*The living room of a Jewish home.*

(As the curtain goes up Esther is seen adjusting a screen in a corner of the room, with David nearby and the other children at a little distance, looking on.)

ESTHER: There! Grandma can't see it now. *(Stands off at a distance to inspect her work.)* Now, David, I'll tell you how we'll do it. When I wink—like this—(Makes laughable distortions of her face in a vain effort to wink.)*

LEO: Aw, look at that!—Such a big girl and can't even wink! Watch me! *(Winks a few times.)* And I can whistle, too! *(Puckers his lips and tries ineffectually.)*

DAVID: Look out, Leo, you'll blow your head off!

ESTHER: Oh, Leo, you'll spoil everything! Grandma might come in any minute now. Now, do listen: When I wink—like this—you get ready, David, to help me take the screen away, and then we'll all jump up and down in front of the tree—

HELEN: Like real, live Indians!

ESTHER: Oh, stupid, what do you think? Think this is an Indian war dance? Don't you know it's Christmas! Now, listen! We'll all jump up and down in front of the tree—solemn-like—and holler: "Surprise! Surprise!"

LEO: I'm going to holler as loud as a—a firecracker—just like this! *(Shouts at the top of his voice.)* "Surprise! Surprise!"

DAVID: I'll bet you'll spoil everything—you always do!

HELEN: What will we do now?

LEO: I know, let's hang our stockings!

HELEN: Yes, yes, let's.

DAVID: Aw, there ain't no Santa Claus!

HELEN: Yes there is.

LEO: I know there is. I seen him!

HELEN: You did? Where?

LEO: In a picture book.

DAVID: Pooh!

ESTHER: Well, who cares, anyhow—as long as we get our stockings filled. I'm going to hang mine.

LEO: Me, too!

HELEN: Me, too!

(All run to fireplace to hang stockings nearby.)

DAVID *(Seating himself pompously in chair and looking disdainfully wise.)*: Pooh! Don't you think I know who really fills those stockings?

(The children are busy hanging their stockings at the fireplace when the door opens, admitting the mother and the grandmother. The children run boisterously toward the door, crying: "Grandmother! Grandmother!")

GRANDMA: My dear, sweet children! How good it feels to hold you in my arms again.

MOTHER: Children, don't smother Grandma!

GRANDMA: My dear Esther, how big you've grown! And David, I declare, you're almost a man! My, my, is it possible five years could make such a change in my dear little grandchildren! And Helen, you're the image of your mother. That's just the way she used to look in my arms long years ago! And Leo, where is he—where is my baby grandchild?

LEO *(On the floor at Grandma's grip, trying to open it.)*: What did you bring me, Grandma?

MOTHER: Shame on you, Leo!

GRANDMA: Never mind, my little cherub, grandma didn't forget you! And it's something that's going to make you just so happy! No, I won't tell you now! You must wait until my trunk comes. And there's something beautiful for Esther and David and Helen. O, won't we all be happy tomorrow when the trunk comes!

HELEN: Santa Claus is going to bring us something, too.

GRANDMA: Santa Claus! But, my dears, Jewish children have no Santa Claus! *(Looks reproachfully at her daughter.)*

HELEN: Oh, yes they have, grandma! You just get up tonight, when it's pitch black, and you'll see him. Oh, he's such a funny little man, with great, big, long whiskers, and he's got a great, big bag full of dolls and candy and bicycles and—and—oh, just everything in the world!

LEO: I seen him, grandma! Yes, I did.

MOTHER *(Apologetically.)*: The children begged so, mother, and it gives them such pleasure!

GRANDMA: And what about Hanukkah!

LEO *(Who has been stirring uneasily near the screen.)*: Esther, you know! you know!

ESTHER: O hush, Leo. You'll spoil everything! *(Makes same distortions of face as she edges near screen.)*

MOTHER: My dear child, what are you making such fearful faces for!

(By this time David has helped Esther to remove the screen, whereupon the children dance and cry: "Surprise! Surprise!" revealing apparently a Christmas tree set in an alcove of the room, off stage. The tree is not seen by the audience.)

GRANDMA: A Christmas tree!—*(An involuntary outburst.)* Children, is this a Jewish home?

LEO: We've got something for you, too, grandma—but I ain't going to tell!

HELEN: Let's get it now, mother dear—please!

ESTHER: Oh, yes, please—p-l-e-a-s-e!

MOTHER: But I thought you were going to surprise grandma.

DAVID: Well, Leo has told her already, hasn't he? Can't expect that little mutt to keep a secret!

MOTHER: David!—Such a way of talking!

(The children press their mother with—"please, please.")

MOTHER: Well, all right, children. Run along now, but be careful— don't muss the other things. *(The children scamper for the door pell-mell.)* I declare, I never saw such spoiled children. They always get just what they want!

GRANDMA: But how could you give them this? *(With a sweeping gesture toward stockings and tree.)* You never saw such things in your home when you were a child! What sort of a Jewish home can this be!

MOTHER: Oh, the children begged so! And you've no idea how happy these harmless little things make them! For they are harmless. The children don't know what they mean. All they know is that Santa Claus fills their stockings with goodies and the tree makes everything look so bright and beautiful.

GRANDMA: But to the world these things stand for the birth of the Christian God!

MOTHER: Now, mother, you know these things aren't going to make my children believe in the Christian God!

GRANDMA: Well, will they help them to believe in the Jewish God?

MOTHER *(With a shrug of the shoulders.)*: As much as most Jews nowadays believe in Him!

GRANDMA: What else can you expect when we are raising a new generation of Jews on things that make good Christians!

MOTHER: Oh, mother, you're so old-fashioned!

GRANDMA: Old-fashioned! It seems to be a crime nowadays to be that! If I won't set up a tree that used to be, and in some dark lands still is, a sign of blood and woe to our people, then I'm old-fashioned!

MOTHER: But, mother, we're not living in the dead past! We're living in a time of tolerance and in this blessed land of liberty.

GRANDMA: All the more reason why we should be loyal to the God of our Fathers who has shielded us and guided us to this day. You find so much delight in celebrating Christmas for the children—why don't you celebrate Hanukkah?

MOTHER: Hanukkah? Who keeps Hanukkah? I have Jewish neighbors and I have not heard the mention of Hanukkah for years! We live so far from the Temple—and besides, nobody goes these days!

GRANDMA: But don't the children go to the Sunday School?

MOTHER: Oh, they study so hard all week and they beg so to sleep and play on Sunday! I just let them have their way. Oh, they'll grow up to be good men and women—you needn't fear!

GRANDMA: God grant it! But you know how proud your father was of his name—his Jewish name—and he told me more than once how happy and proud he would be if his dear little grandchildren would keep up that name. God took him before he could see that his little grandchildren were celebrating Christmas on Hanukkah and didn't even know that it was Hanukkah or what Hanukkah meant!

(The door opens with a loud noise; the children come filing in, one behind the other, each with a gift in his outstretched arms. Esther comes first—hands her gift to Grandma, bows ceremoniously and says:)

ESTHER: A beautiful muff, from your loving grandchild Esther.

(David comes next, bows low like Esther and says:)

DAVID: A beautiful box of handkerchiefs, from your loving grandchild David.

(Then Helen comes—goes through the same business and says:)

HELEN: A beautiful hatpin, from your loving grandchild Helen.

(Leo comes last, with a big box held precariously in his extended arms; he stumbles as he nears Grandma, and the box goes flying out of his hands. David cries out in wrath.)

DAVID: I told you so!

(Leo tries to pick the box up, and answers, tearfully.)

LEO: Well, I couldn't help it!

(Grandma hastens to him and puts her arms around him and says:)

GRANDMA: Never mind, my dear; you have got the loveliest present of all!

(Leo's face breaks into a radiant smile—then he looks from one to the other of the children with helpless appeal and says:)

LEO: I forgot what to say.

(There is general laughter.)

MOTHER: Now, children, you've seen grandma and given her the presents, and it's time to go to bed.

ESTHER: Oh, mother, please let us stay up just a little while yet!

DAVID: There it is!—Bed, bed—as soon as our fun starts!

LEO *(Throws himself flat on the floor in an outburst of temper and cries out.)*: Won't go to bed! Won't go to bed!

MOTHER: Children, I'm ashamed of you! Such behavior!—And before grandma, too!

GRANDMA: There, there, children, you'll do what mother wants you to, I'm sure. I always think of you as such good little children.

LEO *(Goes up to Grandma with a roguish look on his face.)*: I can be the goodest boy in the world, can't I, grandma?

GRANDMA: I'm sure of it, my dear child!

LEO: Then won't you tell us a story?—Just a wee, tiny story—and we'll go to bed.

(The other children press around Grandma and plead: "Yes, yes, a story; please tell us a story!" Grandma looks undecidedly at Mother.)

MOTHER: If grandma wants to—but remember, you must go to bed as soon as she finishes!

(Children cry eagerly and vociferously: "Yes, yes, yes!")

GRANDMA: I brought you a book with beautiful pictures that tells you about grand things that every Jewish child ought to know. *(Walks to her grip to get the book.)*

HELEN: I know—Christmas pictures!

GRANDMA: Christmas, my dears, is for good little Christian children. My pictures are for good little Jewish children.

LEO: What are they about, grandma?

GRANDMA: About Hanukkah.

HELEN: What a funny name!

LEO: I know a giant who's got a funnier name than that!

DAVID: Aw, Kanuka ain't no giant! It's the Jewish Christmas, ain't it, grandma?

GRANDMA: No, my dears, Jews have no Christmas.

ESTHER: But, grandma, we have a Christmas tree!

GRANDMA: A Christmas tree, my child, is intended to make Christian children happy. Jewish children have Hanukkah to make them happy.

ESTHER: Tell us about it, grandma.

GRANDMA: I'll tell it to you just the way I used to tell it to your mother when she was a little child like you. I'll sit down on this little stool near the fireplace and you all gather about me on the floor—that's the way. Now, mother will lower the light—that's the way—mother has not forgotten, I see, how she used to love to hear a story told. There, now, I'll begin.

(Grandma opens the book; the stage is now dark except for the light that falls from the fireplace and shines on the children and Grandma, and, in part, on Mother. As Grandma opens the book, however, a light goes tip on back, center stage, revealing the tableau representing the picture in the book; a light cheese-cloth stretched across an open doorway with one or two electric lights behind it, is the proper

arrangement. When the lights are out the cheese-cloth over the doorway looks like a part of the room, and the audience cannot see through it while the tableau is being set. At the proper moment the lights go up and the tableau stands revealed. Some screen or curtain arrangement may be used on a less complete stage. The tableau is as follows: A Syrian soldier is erecting an idol. Other soldiers are standing with drawn swords over cowering Jews—another soldier is pointing commandingly to the idol over against an old man with white, flowing beard.)

LEO *(Pointing to the picture in the book and crying out.)*: There's Santa Claus!

GRANDMA: No, my dear, that is a brave old man—Mattathias is his name—who would rather die than turn away from the God of Israel.

HELEN *(Pointing to the idol.)*: What a funny looking thing—looks just like a Billikin!

GRANDMA: That's an idol. You know what an idol is—it is what the heathens worshipped in place of God. The Jews, you know, would not worship anyone except the true and only God. Well, there was a bad king—Antiochus was his name—and he was a tyrant, and he sent his soldiers to make the Jews worship that idol. He offered that old man ever so many gifts if he would set the example to his people and bow down to the idol.

ESTHER: Oh, I hope he didn't do it!

GRANDMA: No, my child, he was true to God, as Jews have been for so many hundreds of years!

ESTHER: Well, what did he do?

(The picture darkens and vanishes as Grandma partly closes the book.)

GRANDMA: He cried out in the very face of the drawn sword: "God forbid that we should forsake the law and depart from our faith either to the right or to the left!" And many followed him, so that they became an army to fight even to the death for their Temple and their God!

DAVID: Gee, I wish I'd 'a lived then! I'd 'a just gone out against those—what do you call 'em?—

GRANDMA: Syrians.

DAVID: That's it—and licked the life out of 'em!

LEO: What's next, grandma? Let me turn the page.

(As he turns the page another tableau is revealed. Boys are lying prostrate, soldiers are standing over them with drawn swords; a few Jews are standing about with heads bent with horror and grief; a woman kneels in the midst of the prostrate boys and her head and hands are uplifted to heaven in an attitude of exalted martyrdom.)

HELEN: Oh, what a sad picture!

ESTHER: Are the boys dead, grandma?

LEO: The soldiers killed them, didn't they, grandma?

GRANDMA: Yes, my children, the boys are dead, and the soldiers killed them, and that woman there with her hands lifted up to heaven is their mother.

DAVID: Are they all her boys, grandma?

GRANDMA: All her boys.

ESTHER: Hasn't she any left?

GRANDMA: She has none left.

ESTHER: Well, grandma, what is she going to do?

GRANDMA: God knows!

LEO: Why don't God strike those bad soldiers dead?—I would!

HELEN: Oh, grandma, that's so sad I could cry! Please close the book and tell us about it. *(She pushes the book shut and the picture vanishes.)*

GRANDMA: That woman's name is Hannah, and the soldiers are killing her boys who are faithful to the God of Israel. If the mother had pleaded with her boys to worship the idols perhaps their lives might have been spared.

ESTHER: Oh, grandma, I wish she had done it! I would have done anything to save my boys!

GRANDMA: So would I, my dear, but not so Hannah; she was a martyr.

HELEN: What's that?

DAVID: I know, Joan of Arc was a martyr, wasn't she?

ESTHER: And so was Abraham Lincoln.

GRANDMA: Yes, my children, but you didn't know that we Jews had martyrs, too, did you? For hundreds and hundreds of years we have been suffering sorrow and death in the name of God!

ESTHER: But *we're* not, grandma, and *we're* Jews.

GRANDMA: We may thank God that we are living in this great land of peace and liberty. But there are other lands where Jews are still suffering like martyrs—even in this very hour.

LEO: What's next, grandma?

(A tableau is revealed as Grandma opens the book to another picture. In the center is an altar; on the altar is a shining vessel out of which smoke is rising—the smoke of incense. A priest is standing by the altar with his hand resting on the vessel of incense. A little to the side is a pedestal on which stands a lighted Menorah; a priest is removing his hand from the last light of the Menorah as though he has just lit

it. Two or three more priests are standing near the altar, one with a cornet to his lips, one with cymbals in his hands. In the rear a few Jews are worshipping with their faces almost to the floor. In the foreground stands Judah Maccabee in a commanding attitude.)

HELEN: What's that, grandma?

GRANDMA: That's the dedication of the altar. That's what Hanukkah means—dedication. The very first thing that the Jews did after they won a great victory was to cleanse the Temple of the defilements of the heathen and to hallow it anew for the service of God. That is a new altar you see there on which a priest is burning incense. And that is a new Menorah on which a priest has just lit the lights.

LEO: What's that brass band there for?

GRANDMA: Those are priests, Leo, playing songs of praise and thanksgiving to God.

HELEN: And what are those men doing with their faces to the ground?

GRANDMA: That is the way men worshipped God in those days.

DAVID: And who is that big man in front?

(Picture vanishes as Grandma closes book.)

GRANDMA: Judah Maccabee.

DAVID: Who was he?

GRANDMA: He was one of the sons of Mattathias—the biggest and the bravest of them all. His name comes from letters that he carried on his banner and which stand for the words, "Who is like unto thee, O God, among the mighty?" He won glorious victories and drove the enemy out of the sacred land of Israel.

DAVID: Judah was sure a great man. He was as great as George Washington, for he saved his country, too!

GRANDMA: He did more than that. He saved the Jewish religion. There would have been no Christmas tree if it hadn't been for Judah—for the religion of Christ came from the religion of the Jew.

LEO: What's next, grandma? Oh, there's only one more picture!

GRANDMA: Yes, and you'll like that one best of all.

HELEN: Please let us see it, too!

(Grandma opens the book wide and a tableau is revealed. Nine little children are standing behind a little table on which rests a Hanukkah candlestick containing eight candles, unlighted, and a place for the Shammas, which is in the hand of the first child.)

ESTHER: Oh, look at the little children! Aren't they cute!

DAVID: Are they Judah's children?

GRANDMA: Oh, dear, no! But when Judah was celebrating his great victories and thanking God for the wonderful deliverance, and the priests were relighting the lights in the Temple—for the heathen had put them out—Judah and the congregation ordered that every year at this time Jews in all parts of the world should celebrate these days in gladness and joy. And that is what we call Hanukkah.

HELEN: I wish we kept Kanuka!

GRANDMA: We shall this year, and I hope after this every year.

ESTHER: What are the children saying? Is that it—under the picture?

GRANDMA: Yes. I'll read it to you, soft and low, and you can imagine that you are hearing the children really saying it.

(The first child, holding the lighted Shammas, now steps forward one step and recites:)

FIRST CHILD: This is the Shammas light. It serves to kindle all the other lights. The Bible says: "The memory of the righteous shall be for a blessing." May we live to serve and thus bring light into the lives of others.

(The first child now steps back and hands the Shammas to the second child, who steps one step forward and lights the first candle on the candlestick and recites its part as given below. The second child then hands the Shammas to the third child, who steps forward and lights the second candle, and so on.)

SECOND CHILD: This is the first light. It is the light of our faith. The Bible says God called Israel to be "for a light of the nations." May we do what we can to keep this light burning forever and ever.

THIRD CHILD: This is the second light. It is the light of worship. The Bible says: "Worship the Lord in the beauty of holiness." May we always be faithful in visiting the houses of worship and in carrying out its noble teachings.

FOURTH CHILD: This is the third light. It is the light of justice. The Bible says: "Let justice flow like water and righteousness like a mighty stream." God grant that the day may be at hand when the strong will no longer oppress the weak and men will be upright and fair with one another.

FIFTH CHILD: This is the fourth light. It is the light of charity. The Bible says: "Blessed is he that considereth the poor; the Lord will deliver him in the day of evil." May we always be open of hand and tender of heart to the poor and unfortunate.

SIXTH CHILD: This is the fifth light. It is the light of learning. The Bible says of him who studies in the Torah: "And he shall be like a tree planted by streams of water that bringeth forth its fruit in season and whose leaf doth not wither." Our forefathers were filled with a deep love for the study of the Torah. May we keep this high tradition burning in Israel.

SEVENTH CHILD: This is the sixth light. It is the light of cheer. The Bible says: "A merry heart doeth good like a medicine." May God help us to a sweet disposition and fill our hearts with gladness.

EIGHTH CHILD: This is the seventh light. It is the light of thanksgiving. The Bible says: "Give thanks to the Lord for He is good; for His kindness endureth forever." May we be mindful of the thousand little gifts and blessings that come to us day by day, and may we praise Him whose open hand satisfies the needs of the living.

NINTH CHILD: This is the last light. It is the light of sacrifice. The Bible says: "Offer the sacrifice of righteousness and put your trust in the Lord." On this day we are reminded of the sacrifices of our fathers in behalf of their Torah and their God. May the light of their devotion never go out in Israel.

(The picture vanishes.)

ESTHER: Oh, grandma, aren't the words sweet and beautiful.

GRANDMA: Yes, dear, it is all sweet and beautiful if only Jewish children could be made to understand it and love it year by year.

MOTHER: I haven't heard the story for so many years, mother. I can see myself a child again, lying in the light of the fireplace, drinking in the words of the Hanukkah story. And to think that these are now my children!

GRANDMA: So is generation linked to generation by the noble traditions of our faith.

MOTHER: I thought I had forgotten it all, but how it all comes back to me! I can even hear the Hanukkah hymn ringing in my ears.

(From off stage, as though coming from the distance, is heard the singing of the Hanukkah hymn—as the curtain slowly falls.)

The Light That Never Failed:
A Hanukkah Story

"FATHER," pleaded Bennie, "PLEASE LET me light it just once."

Mr. Roth shook his head. "Not today, Bennie. We have no candles small enough for the menorah; besides, you must not light the candles until the first night of Hanukkah."

Bennie pouted a little. When one is a boy of five, living on a farm three miles away from his nearest playmate, it is hard to wait patiently for a new privilege. And until this year Bennie's father had not considered him old enough to light the Hanukkah lights and say the blessing. "How long must I wait till Hanukkah?" he asked with an impatient wriggle, as Mr. Roth replaced the tin menorah he had shown him on the top shelf of the cupboard.

"Just two weeks," Mr. Roth consoled his son. "Suppose we begin to learn the blessing now?"

Bennie nodded eagerly and a few moments later his mother, entering the kitchen, smiled to hear him repeating: "Boruch atto—boruch atto—boruch atto Adonai—and what's the next word, papa?" She put away the jar of butter she had brought up from the cellar and stood for a moment behind Bennie's chair, her hand resting on his curly head.

"He learns easily, doesn't he?" she said a little wistfully. "When he is a little older, perhaps he can go to Hebrew school like his cousins in New York." She sighed, her eyes wandering through the window over the vast white fields. "It is lonely out here, away from all Jews," she murmured half to herself.

Her husband nodded, for he understood how she missed her family and all the neighbors in the crowded Jewish quarter where she had lived until her marriage. He realized, too how hard she found her many farm duties, how easily she became tired these days, when the heavy snow-drifts seemed to shut them off from the outer world and even the postman failed to appear down the unbroken road, bringing their daily Jewish paper and an occasional letter in his bag. But Morris Roth feared to return to the city, for the doctor had warned him that he would never be well so long as he worked in a crowded tailor shop. His brother had lent him enough money to travel west to take up a claim in Dakota; if he lived on the land just a little while longer, the government would give it to him for his own and there would be a secure home for Bennie and his mother. He had learned to love his new free life in the great out-of-doors; he felt he could not bear to go back to the city again; but he grew worried when he noticed how pale and thin his wife had grown, how often she spoke longingly of home. "When I have a little more saved, I will send her back for a visit," he told himself. "Perhaps she can take Bennie with her. If only her cough would be better and she would not get so tired!"

On this bleak December afternoon, Mr. Roth renewed the same old promise to himself as he taught Bennie the blessing for the Hanukkah lights. And yet that evening, as his wife moved about the little kitchen putting the supper dishes away, there was such a fine color in her cheeks and her eyes were so bright that Mr. Roth felt he had been needlessly anxious. But a week later she complained of pains in her chest and throat, and when Bennie wriggled because she dressed him so slowly, she allowed him to finish buttoning his shoes for himself. Bennie was thunder-struck; he was so used to having his mother pet and spoil him that now he just sat on the edge of the bed with his mouth wide-open, too astonished even to protest when his mother lay back on the pillows and said she was too tired to dress him. When Mr. Roth came in from milking, she tried to laugh away her faintness, but he was badly frightened. He dressed Bennie as well as he could and awkwardly set the table for breakfast and heated some coffee. He would not allow Mrs. Roth to get up again, although he promised not to go for the doctor if she felt any better the next day.

The next morning Mrs. Both tried to drag herself about the house, but by noon she was back in bed again, looking so white and weak that even Bennie was frightened. He stood watching his father with great round eyes as Mr. Roth pulled on his heavy boots and sweater, and moved nervously about the kitchen preparing for a trip to town ten miles away. Bennie went to the window and scratched a little hole in the frosted pane.

"Papa," he announced, "you can't go to town today. There aren't any roads. It's all white and smooth just like a table cloth."

Mr. Roth's lips tightened. "I've got to make a road, Bennie boy," he said simply. "I'll take a shovel along and dig my way through." He followed Bennie to the window and looked from the white prairies to the grey clouds over head with troubled eyes. "If the blizzard only holds off a while longer," he muttered more to himself than to Bennie, "I'll get the doctor back here. But if we're held up in the snow—"

"Is mama very sick?" Bennie asked him.

"I'm afraid so." His father pulled on his heavy fur mittens. "So you must be a very good boy and take care of her until I get back. Don't worry her and if she doesn't want to talk to you, just let her rest. I'll bring you some candy from town and," with sudden inspiration, "if you're a good boy all afternoon, I'll let you light the candles and say the blessing tonight."

Bennie clapped his hands gleefully. "Tonight's Hanukkah, tonight's Hanukkah," he chanted shrilly. "Boruch atto Adonai—please hear me say the blessing before you go, papa." But his father kissed him hastily and started for the door. "Tonight, when you light the candles," he promised. "But now I must go for the doctor right away."

Feeling strangely frightened, although he hardly knew why, Bennie followed his father to the bedroom, where his mother lay tossing upon the bed. Her face was flushed and she threw her head about on the pillow. But she tried to smile when she saw that Bennie drew back afraid.

"It's just my throat," she managed to whisper. "I don't seem to be able to breathe. But I'll get along all right till you come back," she ended bravely. "Just leave something on the table for Bennie's supper. And, Bennie, please don't come in and bother mama for a little while. Play out in the kitchen and let her sleep."

A few moments later Bennie stood in the middle of the kitchen, feeling very much alone. The rapidly rising wind howled and blustered until the frail little house seemed to shake before it; then the howling would cease for a moment and all would grow so quiet that it seemed as though he were the only living person in the world. The little fellow wanted to run to his mother, as he always did, for comfort; then he remembered that he was a big boy now, big enough to take care of mother and the farm, when, father was away. He squared his shoulders resolutely as he went to the cupboard for his box of toys.

There were only a few playthings: the tin soldiers his Aunt Minna had sent him for his birthday, a rubber ball which had refused to bounce properly after he had pricked it with a pin, a box of dominoes, excellent for building forts for his soldiers, and several picture books. For a while he amused himself turning the pages and murmuring the stories his mother had told him so often that he knew them by heart. There was Golden-locks in a blue dress and red sunbonnet driven home by three angry bears; on the next page Cinderella rode to the ball behind six prancing white horses and here was Jack climbing the beanstalk which grew beside his mother's cottage door. Best of all were the pictures in the largest story book, pictures of a little boy named Joseph, with a kind father and wicked brothers, who stole his pretty coat and threw him into a cave. Bennie studied the pictures with satisfaction, especially the one of Joseph sitting in a big chair with a great many people fanning him or bowing before him. But soon he found that it was growing too dark to see the pictures distinctly; the short December day had deepened into twilight and the room was gray with misty lights, while the great stove in the corner cast queer flickering shadows on the walls.

The boy walked to the window to raise the blinds and again scratched a peep hole in the frosty pane. It was snowing hard, great white flakes that whirled and danced like bits of torn paper. Bennie shivered a little as he hoped his father would be home soon; he knew daddy was a big, strong man, but it was not good to think of him out there in the darkness. He wondered what time it was, anyhow. There was a clock in the bedroom and if mother was awake she would be glad to tell him, he reasoned. He stole softly to her bed. In the uncertain light he could see that her eyes were closed; she seemed to be asleep, but she made queer sounds like some one crying and her breast rose and fell jerkily beneath the blankets.

Bennie tiptoed back into the kitchen, curled himself up on the sofa and wondered what to do next. He had been taught not to be afraid of the dark, but he did want to go on looking at his picture books and playing with his soldiers. Besides, he was beginning to feel hungry and he was sure he wouldn't enjoy the supper of bread and milk and pie father had left on the table, if he had to eat it in the dark. But ever since he could remember, both father and mother had forbidden him to light the lamps. He wondered whether they would care tonight, when he was such a big boy, old enough to light the Hanukkah candles.

Suddenly he jumped to his feet. Hadn't father said, just before he left, that tonight was Hanukkah! Then he must light his candles right away, for hadn't father explained to him, while learning the blessing, that he must kindle the first yellow taper and say the strange Hebrew words just as soon as it got dark on the first night of Hanukkah? Bennie didn't understand just why he wasn't allowed to light the lamps, but would be permitted to light the Hanukkah candles; nor did he consider how worried his parents would be to have him striking matches unless they stood near to watch him. It was enough for him that it was Hanukkah at last and that he knew the difficult blessing over the light, every word of it. Why, he wouldn't have to awaken poor mother to help him, which relieved him a good deal, as he felt somehow that she would get well quicker if she were allowed to sleep as long as she pleased. But how could he reach the menorah father had put away on the very top shelf, next to the candle sticks for Shabbas? Bennie was not easily daunted. Even if he couldn't use the menorah the first night, he was determined hot to be cheated out of lighting the very first candle tonight. He couldn't reach the box of little yellow tapers that father had put away with the menorah, but on the lowest shelf he found just what he wanted—an old tin candlestick with a half-burned candle which mother sometimes used when she went down into the cellar and didn't care to bother with a lamp.

Mrs. Roth always kept the box of matches well out of the reach of Bennie's active fingers, so he didn't trouble himself to look for them. Taking the candle he opened the stove door and thrust it into the flames. Walking very carefully, for lie felt mother might consider what he was doing almost as naughty as playing with fire, he put the candle back into the holder and set it upon the window sill. Then, standing very straight, he slowly repeated the Hebrew benediction: "Boruch atto Adonoi Elohenu Melech ho-olom asher kiddeshonu bemitzvosov vetzivonu lehadlik ner shel Hanukkah."

Sitting on the floor in the warm patch of light cast by the stove, Bennie ate his supper, looking proudly all the while at his candle burning fine and straight in the window. When the dishes were all empty, he went to the window pane and amused himself by scraping off the frost with the kitchen knife. He wanted to see his candle throwing a pretty ribbon of light on the snow; he knew it would look nice, for he remembered how pretty the lamp in the kitchen window had appeared to him one night when they had come from town and had seen it shining as they drove up the hill. He wanted his candle to shine a long ways—just like a lamp— and, bringing out an old lantern which his father had once given him to play with, he set the light within it and again placed it before the carefully scraped pane. Then he sat down on the window sill, watching the snow flurries and wishing for father to come home.

Father came at last, bringing with him a tall, bearded man who carried a little black satchel and hurried into mother's room without saying a word. Father went after him and for a time Bennie sat trembling besides his Hanukkah light, wondering what it was all about. After a very little while, although it seemed to Bennie that he had waited all night, father came back into the kitchen and took the little fellow in his arms. Bennie saw that he was crying and it frightened him, for he had never seen his father cry before.

"Is mama very sick?" he asked.

"The doctor says she will get well," answered Mr. Roth, and his voice trembled. "You can't understand it all, Bennie boy, but there was something bad in her throat," and he added something about diphtheria which meant nothing to Bennie, who just considered it one of the big words grown-up people were always using to confuse him. "But the doctor has just burned it all out and she will get well. Only if we hadn't come in time—" He stopped and shuddered. "Bennie, if you hadn't put your light in the window we might have been an hour later in getting here and then the doctor says it would have been too late. Our lanterns went out at the top of the hill and the snow was so blinding that we might have floundered about half the night before we found the house. But your little candle helped us to find the way."

"I said the blessing all right," Bennie told his father, "but was it all right not to use the regular menorah and a yellow candle?" he ended anxiously.

"You did just the right thing," his father assured him.

But Bennie was not satisfied. "Please, papa," he pleaded, "please get down the real menorah and the yellow candle and let me light it and say the Hebrew for you. Please!"

Smiling a little uncertainly, Mr. Both brought down the tin menorah and the box of yellow tapers. He gave Bennie one for the shammas, explaining that it was to light the others, and watched him with the same twisted smile as the child adjusted and lit the first candle. "Boruch atto Adonoi," began Bennie proudly, and he wondered why his father hid his face in his hands and started to cry all over again.

HANUKKAH SKETCH

CHARACTERS

Father Time
A Child
Hannah, and Her Seven Sons
Mattahias
Judas Maccabee
Crowd of Israelites: Warriors, women, and children

SCENE—*A large room. A table stands at one side (left), at which sits old Father Time, writing in a large hook. He has his hourglass and scythe at his side. Books and papers in great disorder cover the table. Two doors, right and left.*

(The Child enters at the right door, and goes left. He and Father Time remain seated at the table, while the characters are on and off the stage.)

FATHER TIME *(Writes busily.)*: Dear me, dear me! Here it is almost New Year again, and I've not half my accounts written. I've gotten so confused with these discoveries of the North Pole and airships that it seems as though I'll never catch up with my days. Let me see. *(Writes hurriedly, consulting his calendar every few minutes.)*

(A knock is heard at the door.)

FATHER TIME *(Testily, keeping on writing.)*: What is it? Don't come in, I'm busy.

(Door opens and Child enters, big-eyed with wonder, but perfectly at ease.)

FATHER TIME *(Continues writing.)*: Well, what do you want?

(No answer.)

FATHER TIME *(Pounds on the table.)*: Hurry up, I say! Can't you see I'm busy?

(Child jumps.)

(Father Time looks up for the first time and sees Child.)

FATHER TIME *(Kindly.)*: Oh, hello, I didn't mean to frighten you!

CHILD *(Politely.)*: You didn't, sir. I'm a Jew, you know, and we never get scared.

FATHER TIME: Indeed! Well, and what do you want here, my little man?

CHILD *(Advances to the table.)*: Please, sir, are you Father Time?

FATHER TIME: That's what the earth people call me.

CHILD: Then I want you to show me where all the stories come from.

FATHER TIME *(Astonished.)*: What!

CHILD *(Repeats.)*: I want you to tell me a story. When Mother put me to bed tonight she said that Father Time kept all the stories locked up in his books. So I thought I'd come and see for myself. Is this one? *(He reaches out for the book nearest him, and tries to open it.)*

FATHER TIME: Hold on, hold on there, my young man. That book is not to be opened by anyone but me.

CHILD: Oh, excuse me. But why can't I do it?

FATHER TIME: Because that's the Book of the Future, and no man may look into that. But there, there. *(He glances at his hourglass.)* I've a few minutes to spare now, and I'll show you some of the pictures in this other book. Come!

(Child climbs on his knee. Father Time unclasps a large volume bound in dark colors.)

CHILD: What is this one called?

FATHER TIME: The Book of the Past.

CHILD: Did you write it?

FATHER TIME: Yes, my boy.

CHILD *(Peers in as Father Time turns the pages absent-mindedly.)*: How funny it looks! And what queer kind of ink you have used—it is so faint.

FATHER TIME: Ah, my dear, that is memory. But now, we must hurry to our story. What kind do you want?

CHILD *(Eagerly.)*: Oh, fairy stories, please!

FATHER TIME: You won't find them in here or at least men don't give them that name. *(He ponders a moment.)* But wait, I've an idea! Can you tell me what holiday is coming next?

CHILD *(Proudly.)*: Hanukkah, sir.

FATHER TIME *(Nodding assent.)*: That's right. So now, I am going to introduce you to some of the people who made that festival for you and let them tell their own story.

(Father Time turns back page after page, stopping at the one he wants, and bids the Child look down at it. Instantly, the light of the stage grows dimmer, and figures advance from the shadows at the back of the stage. The light brightens again, and shows Hannah surrounded by her seven sons.)

HANNAH *(Looks down at them lovingly, and fondles the youngest.)*: Oh, my sons, my own fine boys, do you know how dear you are to your mother Hannah?

FIRST BOY: Yes, Mother, but you have taught us something better than that.

SECOND BOY: Aye, to love and serve the God of Israel, blessed be He!

SEVENTH and SMALLEST BOY: Oh, Mother, do you think I'll ever get the chance to keep my promise? I am ready to die.

HANNAH *(Takes him in her arms impulsively.)*: Hush, child, hush! You know not whereof you speak!

THIRD BOY *(Interrupts.)*: Oh, no Mother. He does know what it means to worship the God of Israel, when all our enemies try to make us sacrifice to their strange gods.

FOURTH BOY: Aye, were we not stoned in the street yesterday, as we hurried home from the Temple!

FIFTH BOY *(Timidly.)*: Mother, think you harm can come of it all?

HANNAH *(Looks frightened, and tries to gather them all into her arms. Then she assumes a brave air and says)*: No fear, no one need fear, as long as he remains true to his trust. Come, my sons; once more let us pledge ourselves to the worship of the Most High—blessed be He!

(They all stand in a circle and raise their hands, chanting.)

We swear to be true to the God of our Fathers,
To the truth that Jehovah to Israel has shown;
We sing loud His praise, with our voices we raise—

(Sounds of tumult outside interrupt.)

SIXTH BOY: Mother, Mother, the time has come!

(He runs out of the room, the others following him.)

HANNAH *(Hurries after them sobbing frantically.)*: My children, my sons, my children! Come back, come back!

(Pause of a few moments.)

CHILD *(Gazing up at Father Time, piteously.)*: And were they all killed?

FATHER TIME: Yes, yes, my dear. But look here, *(points to the next page)* here is a happier story.

(Stage darkens again. Music plays a triumphal march. The stage brightens, showing Judas Maccabee in warrior costume. He stands in the center of the stage, with his helmet off, paying reverence to his father who is dressed in the garments of a High Priest. Warriors, women, and children stand around.)

JUDAS MACCABEE: Give my thy blessing, my father!

MATTATHIAS: You have conquered the enemy, slain the foe. The great and the mighty your arm has laid low.

JUDAS Maccabee: In the name of the Lord, I triumphed over them.

MATTATHIAS: The Assyrian's army all lie in the dust. Forever and ever their heavy swords rust.

JUDAS Maccabee: The Almighty, blessed be He, hath cast out his foe!

MATTATHIAS: Israel's freedom through you is rewon, Jehovah's best blessing be on you, my son!

CHORUS *(All chant.)*:
> Hail to the conqueror.
> Hail to the Maccabee:
> He who has saved Israel,
> He who has destroyed the enemy.
> He who will lead Israel among the nations;
> Hail, all hail!

(They form a procession and file out of the room, Judas Maccabee and Mattathias leading.)

(Pause.)

CHILD: Oh, that was fine! Show me some more, please. *(He tries to hide his yawns, but begins to look very tired.)*

FATHER TIME: Aha, I think I had better look at my hour glass! Somebody is sleepy; it is high time that he should be in bed!

CHILD *(Rubbing his eyes.)*: I'm not tired, honest I'm not! *(Yawns again.)*

FATHER Time *(Laughs good-naturedly.)*: Well, I am. So goodnight.

(Child begins to slip down from Father Timers knees and as he does so the room darkens again.)

CHILD *(Sleepily.)*: Goodnight! Thank you, Father Time.

(Chorus outside sings the traditional Hanukkah Hymn while curtain falls.)

A Make-Believe Hanukkah:
A Play for Children in Three Acts

CHARACTERS

Mrs. Berg

Millie
Albert } her children
Gertrude

Sarah
Dinah } women of Modin
Hannah

Mattathiah, a priest of Modin

Judah
Simeon } his sons

Nicander, a Syrian general

A Messenger

Soldiers of the Syrian Army

Soldiers of the Maccabees

A Hebrew Captive of Modin

Amanda, a society girl of Modin

Hymander, a club man of Modin

Scene of Play—*The Living room in the Home of the Bergs, for the Prolog.*

Acts I, II, and III— *A Street Scene in Modin.*

Time—*Present Day for Prolog;*
165 Before Common Era for Acts I, II, and III.

Prolog

SCENE—*Mrs. Berg's Living room.*
TIME—*A Sunday afternoon in December.*
CURTAIN—*Mrs. Berg is seated at a table reading a Sunday paper. Pause.*

(The pause is broken by a drum beat. Enter Millie, Gertrude and Albert, marching in military fashion.)

MRS. BERG: Please, please, children, do not make so much noise. Don't you know this is Sunday?

ALBERT: This isn't our Sunday, mama. It's our Monday, and we can play soldier if we want to on our Monday. *(Beats drum.)*

MRS. BERG: No, no. You are mistaken. Today is Sunday for all of us in America, and we must be very particular not to disturb our neighbors. Can't you find some other way of amusing yourselves?

MILLIE: But we want to play soldier, mama.

GERTRUDE: Please, mama, let us play soldier. We won't make any noise.

MRS. BERG: But you can't play soldier without making a great deal? There's the drumming, and then the shooting. Why, in warfare the noise is deafening.

GERTRUDE: Oh, mama, you must be the Red Cross nurse and wear a white cap.

MRS. BERG: Why should I be a Red Cross nurse? We're longer at war, thank God!

GERTRUDE: Oh, this is only a make-believe war, and in war somebody is always killed and you got to nurse them.

MRS. BERG: What a horrible game! It's bad enough for men to kill one another in the name of war but for children to make-believe war is terrible. Where did you get that notion?

ALBERT: Aw, mama, we're only Hanukkah soldiers.

MRS. BERG: Hanukkah soldiers? There are no Hanukkah soldiers, no more than there are Christmas soldiers.

ALBERT: Yes, there are, mama. Our rabbi said so this morning.

MRS. BERG: But Hanukkah soldiers! Is that what the rabbi called them?

ALBERT: Well, he didn't call them Hanukkah soldiers exactly. He said we celebrate Hanukkah because the Maccabees drove the Syrians out of Palestine and the Maccabees were soldiers.

MRS. BERG: Oh, so that is what you mean.

ALBERT: Now, can we play soldiers?

MRS. BERG: Did the rabbi tell you to play soldier?

MILLIE: No. He said we should remember the Hanukkah soldiers because they were brave.

MRS. BERG: Yes, indeed, they were heroic. But you mustn't call them Hanukkah soldiers. They were called Maccabees.

ALBERT: Were they Jews, mama?

MRS. BERG: Yes, and very good and true. But compared to the Syrians they were few in number.

ALBERT: And is that why we have Hanukkah?

MRS. BERG: Yes, in memory of the brave Maccabees and their followers who overcame the armies of Syria that were ten times, perhaps a hundred times, larger than their own.

MILLIE: Oh, the rabbi didn't tell us that.

MRS. BERG: Oh, yes, I am sure he did. But you didn't pay attention.

GERTRUDE: You tell us, mama. Tell us about Hanukkah.

ALBERT: Yes, mama. I like to hear you tell us a story.

MILLIE: Please, mama; we won't make any noise.

MRS. BERG: I suppose you have heard the story of Hanukkah many times.

GERTRUDE: But it always sounds new. Will you tell us?

MRS. BERG: Then listen. *(The children squat on the floor near her chair.)* The festival we call Hanukkah is celebrated because of what happened many, many years ago, when our Jewish ancestors lived in Palestine. In this war Syria won and, growing ambitious, took Palestine. The inhabitants objected, but were too feeble to throw off the yoke at first. Gradually the oppression of the Syrians became intolerable, especially when the Syrian King, Antiochus IV, compelled the people to abandon their religion and worship the god of the Greeks whom the Syrians had accepted. In those days, children, everything Greek was fashionable. If anybody wanted to be in style he spoke Greek, wore Greek clothes and imitated the habits and practices of the Greek people, even worshipping the pagan god, Zeus, instead of the Eternal Creator of heaven and earth. Of course, many of the Jews in those days wanted to be in fashion and speak only Greek and worship in the popular Greek temples, so it was not easy to make all the people of Palestine turn against the Syrians. But the rulers of Syria were not content to let well enough alone. They became insolent. They compelled the people of Palestine to do their bidding. They insulted, scoffed and abused. They even killed those who resisted, no matter whom it happened to be, old or young, man, woman or child. The Jews endured it as long as they could, and when the Syrians insisted on the Jews worshipping their false gods and imitating their wicked practices, a priest of Israel living in a little town of Modin, not far from Jerusalem, rallied his people about him and defied the commands of the king. The Syrian soldiers tried to arrest him, but he overpowered them and a revolt broke out which resulted in a war lasting four years. Finally Palestine was rid of the Syrian tyrants and the country freed. The Maccabees became rulers and the people prospered. In commemoration of this great victory we celebrate Hanukkah.

ALBERT: What was the name of the general who conquered the Syrians?

MRS. BERG: Judah, called the Maccabee. He and his four brothers, after the death of their father, led the armies of Israel to victory. They removed the pagan images from the Temple and rededicated it to the worship of the one and only God.

ALBERT: Mama, did they have airships?

MRS. BERG: Oh, no. They had very few weapons, possibly bows and arrows and lances. But it wasn't their weapons alone. They were fired by an undying love for their God and their country.

ALBERT: Mama, I wish we could be soldiers like the Maccabees.

GERTRUDE: Oh, let's make believe we are in Palestine and driving out the Syrians.

MILLIE: I want to be a general.

GERTRUDE: You can't be general, Millie. A general is a man. Albert must be General Judah.

MRS. BERG: Now, what are you up to?

GERTRUDE: We are going to play a make-believe Hanukkah.

MRS. BERG: What game is that?

MILLIE: It is not a game, mama. We are going to show you how the Maccabees rose up against the mighty power of Syria.

ALBERT: Will you let us, mama? We won't make much noise.

GERTRUDE: You can be the mama in the play. Her name was Hannah, and she had seven sons, and the Syrian soldiers oh/they were so mean!

MILLIE: You mustn't tell the story. We will act it. May we, mama?

MRS. BERG: Then get your wits together, because you will have to be real clever to make-believe a play like that. I will call your father, so he can see it, too.

Curtain.

ACT I

SCENE—*A Street in Modin.*
TIME—*165 Before Common Era.*
CURTAIN—*A Syrian Messenger crosses stage quickly. Pause.*
Enter Mattathiah, his son, Judah, Simeon, and men of Modin.

MATTATHIAH *(Showing excitement, addressing Judah.)*: Is it true, Judah, that you saw a Syrian messenger pass thru our little town of Modin? This is very unusual. As a rule, messengers of the Syrian army are bound for Jerusalem, seventeen miles to the north of us. This is not a good omen, my friends.

JUDAH: He is the second messenger I have seen this week, father. The day after the Sabbath, while I was leading the flocks into the valley, I saw another messenger of the Syrian army. I thought he was following me, and when I called him, he hurried away.

MATTATHIAH: These Syrians are prowling around here to spy on us. How long are we to endure this?

SIMEON Father, we must drive them out—every Syrian.

JUDAH: There are still strong men in Israel.

MATTATHIAH: It is well that we have brave men among us lest we hang our heads in shame. Ever since the King, Antiochus, returned from Rome he has tried to force us to bend our knees to his pagan Zeus.

JUDAH: What right has he to tell us whom we must worship? Is it not enough that we pay him taxes?

MATTATHIAH: Brave words, my son. Maybe there will yet arise a soldier among us in whom is the spirit of David, the great warrior-king.

JUDAH: The only way to rid Palestine of the Syrian is by the might of the sword.

MATTATHIAH: God forbid. But this is the Sabbath. Only words of peace benefit us. Let us enter the house of prayer. *(They leave. Enter Hymander.)*

HYMANDER: Praise be Zeus! *(Starts exercising.)*

(Enter Amanda.)

AMANDA: Hello, Hyman, what are you doing?

HYMANDER *(Continues his exercises.)*: Going in for athletics. I have been to the gymnasium. Feel my muscle. *(Amanda feels his muscle.)*

AMANDA: By Zeus, you're as strong as Hercules.

HYMANDER: I am entered in the contests of the Greek Athletic Club. There's more fun racing in the stadium than studying Torah in cheder.

AMANDA: Good for you, Hyman. I'm glad to see you are up to date.

HYMANDER: Say, Miriam, don't call me Hyman. That's no longer my name. The court at Jerusalem has granted me the right to call myself Hymander.

AMANDA: Excuse me. But you are not the only camel in the caravan. I have changed my name to Amanda. All the girls in my set are changing their old Hebrew names and speaking only Greek. Father said I could take dancing lessons from a Greek professor, even if I do live in a small town. Do you dance?

HYMANDER: Sure. Suppose I spend all my time in study? All my chums in Jerusalem are going in for Greek fashions. We'll liven things up in this old burg with our new styles. There are too many old fogies here like old man Mattathiah.

AMANDA: And his sons. They are just like him. I should think they would want to know how to dance the new steps. Do you know the new steps?

HYMANDER: If it's a Greek dance I do.

AMANDA: Can you dance the Venus trot?

HYMANDER: Is it like the Pan jazz?

AMANDA: Oh, it's the latest stunt. Come, I will show you.

(They begin dancing. Enter Mattathiah, Judah, Simeon and elders.)

MATTATHIAH: For shame! Do you not know this is the Sabbath?

HYMANDER: Let us alone. What do we care what day it is?

MATTATHIAH: Alas! This desecration of the Sabbath is more to be feared than the armies of Syria. Come, my sons, lest we witness a daughter of our village desecrating the Sabbath.

HYMANDER: Hurry along, old man, or you will lose your way.

JUDAH *(As he lays hold of Hymander.)*: Take that back! No man speaks disrespectfully of my father.

MATTATHIAH *(Separating them.)*: Control your temper, my son.

JUDAH: Does he not know how to respect grey hairs?

MATTATHIAH: Both he and the maid and all those who follow the practices of the Greeks have forsaken the law of Moses. They and their party have divided this country. Were we all followers of the laws of our fathers, the Syrians would fear us. As it is, they know we are not united and can lord it over us like tyrants.

HYMANDER: You're a lot of old fossils. I believe we should obey our King. He commands us to become Greeks, and worship Zeus.

AMANDA: And that is what we are going to do here in Modin.

MATTATHIAH: Hussy, what right have you to talk?

AMANDA: Well, in Greece a woman has a right to her own opinion, and what is good enough for the Greeks is good enough for us. Besides, my father wants me to be in style. He don't believe a woman should grind corn and dry grapes all her life. *(Messenger enters trying to hear the conversation by stealth.)*

MATTATHIAH: I do not like this. Evil betides a country that follows the footsteps of other nations. A house divided against itself cannot stand. The Syrians must go. They are bringing evil ways into Palestine. *(Messenger leaves quickly.)*

HYMANDER: Well, business has been good since the Syrians took hold.

AMANDA: And this town was dead till the Syrians came here.

MATTATHIAH: Come, my sons, our Sabbath was not given us for a street brawl.

(Judah and Simeon leave, also elders.)

HYMANDER: I told him a thing or two.

AMANDA: That old man is the meanest man in town and his son, Judah, is just like him. I don't see what harm it is if we are Greeks instead of Hebrews. Come, take lunch with me, Hymander. My father had some wine sent him from Macedon.

(They leave swinging hands. Enter Messenger. Enter Nicander.)

NICANDER: Did you hear what that old priest said? Messenger Yes, my Lord. He said the Syrians must go.

NICANDER: Old rebel! I will make it hot for him. Of old they were called a stiff-necked race. Now I will show him who is master. But wait, step aside. Here come some women of the town. Let us hear what they have to say.

(Enter Dinah and Sarah.)

DINAH: Woe is me. Our sons are to be taken away from us for soldiers for the accursed Syrians.

SARAH: If we only had brave men in Israel who would throw off this yoke of the oppressor.

DINAH: May our Father, our King, keep war from us.

SARAH: It is the only way to rid ourselves of the Syrians.

(They leave.)

NICANDER: The old gossips don't like us. But I will break their pride and make them acknowledge Antiochus and Zeus. Just watch me!

MESSENGER: Yes, my Lord.

NICANDER: Then go, fetch in the first man you happen to meet. We will force him to acknowledge Zeus and the King. If he resists we will slay him on the spot as an example to the rest of the stiff-necked Hebrews. *(Messenger leaves. Enter soldier dragging Hannah and her son.)*

A SOLDIER: Come on.

HANNAH: You shall not take my boy.

NICANDER: What's all this noise about?

A SOLDIER: This Hebrew woman refuses to let us muster her on. He's drafted for the army.

NICANDER: Drafted? Then he belongs to us. Begone, woman!

HANNAH: No, you shall not take him. Six of my sons have been wrenched from me. He alone is left. No! No! He shall not be led away for slaughter.

NICANDER: Soldier of Antiochus, do your duty! *(He tries to take the boy from Hannah.)*

HANNAH: Rather kill me than take my son.

NICANDER: Off with her. We have no time for woman's tears.

HANNAH: Help! Help! Men of Israel, help!

NICANDER: Be still. How dare you disobey our orders. I am a Syrian general! Do you know what you are doing? You will be killed.

NICANDER: He belongs to us. Soldiers, take him in charge! *(They drag the boy away.)*

HANNAH: Help! Help! *(Hannah follows, calling aloud for help. Enter messenger until man.)*

MESSENGER: My Lord, this man I have captured to make sacrifices to Zeus.

NICANDER: Down on your knees, you Hebrew simpleton. Acknowledge Zeus.

HEBREW OF MODIN: Never!

NICANDER: Kill him!

HEBREW OF MODIN: Pity me, I obey. O, Zeus! *(Bends the knee.)*

(Enter Mattathiah.)

MATTATHIAH: Who calls on the name of Zeus? *(Knocks down the captive.)*

NICANDER: Treason!

MATTATHIAH: To arms! Enough of Syrian tyrants!

Curtain.

ACT II

Scene—*Street in Modin.*
Time—*As Act I.*
Curtain—*Enter Amanda and Hymander.*

AMANDA: What has happened, Hymander? The market is in an uproar. Soldiers are hurrying to and fro and our fellow townsmen are standing about talking instead of going into the fields.

HYMANDER: Perhaps it is another holiday. Every time they feel like loafing they take a day off and call it a festival.

AMANDA: No, you are mistaken this time. The men look too solemn for merriment. Something has happened. Oh, I do hope they have not lost their heads and declared war against Antiochus. It would be just like that old Mattathiah to defy the King and plunge us into war. That would spoil all my fun. You would have to enlist, Hymander.

HYMANDER: Not I. Suppose I would fight Syria? Never. Amanda You would have to fight for Syria or against her.

HYMANDER: Neither. I prefer athletics to war. You get too tanned in the army and sunburn is not fashionable. It makes people think you work.

AMANDA: You must enlist or none of us girls will ever speak to you again. O, I wish I could join the army.

HYMANDER: If you enlisted I'd feel like entering the army

AMANDA: Oh, why wasn't I burn a man!

(A messenger enters.)

HYMANDER *(To the messenger.)*: Hey, messenger, what's the news in Syria?

MESSENGER: King Antiochus orders the revolt suppressed at all cost. *(Messenger leaves quickly.)*

AMANDA: Revolt? Is there really a revolt in Modin? That will make it livelier here than it was during the carnival. Guess I'll postpone my trip to Jerusalem. Did you know there was a revolt, Hyman?

HYMANDER: That's no reason for calling me Hyman. I told you my name is Hymander and if you were in my boots you wouldn't feel so happy. This means war. Guess I'll leave town till the noise blows over. I suppose this is some of that old fogy's doings.

(Enter Dinah, Sarah and Hannah. They walk with bowed heads.)

AMANDA: Peace be unto you, mothers of Israel. Sarah There is no peace. War has been declared.

DINAH *(To Hymander.)*: Why haven't you enlisted? Your country needs you.

HYMANDER: Oh, there are plenty without me. Besides, I am opposed to war with Syria.

HANNAH: For shame! The despoiler who robs us of our sons. Will you defend your country against that robber, Syria?

HYMANDER: Syria hasn't robbed me of anything. I have had more fun since Syria ruled this country than any of us had in the old regime.

SARAH: The desecrator would force us to defile our holy Temple by offering sacrifices to false gods!

HYMANDER: Oh, you people of Modin make too much fuss over trifles. What difference does it make if we worship the God of Israel or Zeus? King Antiochus commands us to follow him. We are his subjects and should obey. It's well enough for you to talk about war. You don't have to fight. But we men do and we don't want war with Syria.

SARAH: If our men will not wipe out the defilement of that mad king Antiochus, then we women and mothers of Israel will tear him to pieces.

AMANDA: Don't count on me. It costs me too much to have my fingernails manicured.

HANNAH: Come, my sisters, we disgrace ourselves talking to these free-thinkers and scoffers. They are more to be feared than the sword of the enemy.

(Dinah, Sarah and Hannah leave.)

AMANDA: I remember the time these women tied grapes in my father's vineyard, and now they consider themselves better than I am, because I have been to Jerusalem and believe it stylish to follow Greek fashions. Idiots. As if these countrywomen could tell me what's what. Come, Hymander, let's go into the market-place and see what's going on there.

(Hymander and Amanda leave. Enter Mattathiah with Hebrew soldiers.)

MATTATHIAH: One, two; one, two; right, left! Right, left! *(The army marches.)* Halt! *(The men stand still.)* No, my men, I tell you it is impossible for me to command you. My eyes are not dim, nor are my natural forces abated. But I am too old to lead you against a powerful army Syria is bringing up against us. War is for youth. A younger man must lead you.

A SOLDIER: Judah, let Judah lead us! Soldiers Judah! Judah!

MATTATHIAH: Judah. my son, stand forth. *(Judah stands out from the ranks.)* Judah, your fellow soldiers elect you captain in my stead. Are you willing to hunger and thirst, to enter the valley of the shadow of death and fear no evil? Will you be strong and courageous?

JUDAH: I will!

MATTATHIAH: 'Tis well. Be as a hammer to smite the foe. *(Transfers his sword to Judah.)* Now lead your countrymen to battle. Restore the holy Temple that vile hands have desecrated. Be brave. The Lord is your light and your salvation, of whom, then, need you be afraid?

JUDAH: Neither men nor princes.

MATTATHIAH: And this is your slogan: Who is like unto Thee among the mighty, O God!

JUDAH: Who is like unto Thee among the mighty, O God!

MATTATHIAH *(Raising his hands as he pronounces the benediction.)*: May God bless thee and keep thee; may God have His countenance shine upon thee and give thee grace; may God lift up His countenance upon thee and send thee peace.

JUDAH: Amen! *(To soldiers.)*: Fall in. Forward, march!

(Mattathiah, Judah, soldiers leave. Enter Nicander followed by messenger.)

NICANDER: Well, now we have gone far enough away from barracks so the officers and soldiers cannot hear what you say. Is it true you bring a message from his royal highness, the prince of peace?

MESSENGER: Yes, my lord. Nicander What does he say?

MESSENGER: His Royal Highness says to put down the revolt that has broken out in this city.

NICANDER: Well, if the king wants the revolt put down, why don't he come here himself and do it?

MESSENGER: Is that your answer to the king?

NICANDER: No, no! Tell the king that if he wants me to put down a revolt among these hard-headed, stiff-necked farmers, he'll have to send me an army of a hundred thousand picked soldiers, every scythe-spoke chariot in his army, his elephant cavalry and then another hundred thousand soldiers and plenty of money to hire mercenaries.

MESSENGER: Yes, my Lord.

NICANDER: And tell the King my vacation is near at hand. Tell him that he should arrange to hire a substitute.

MESSENGER: Yes, my Lord.

NICANDER: And you can tell the king that war is not my business. I am a blacksmith by trade and I am only doing this to accommodate him.

MESSENGER: Yes, my Lord.

(Messenger leaves. Enter Hymander and Amanda.)

HYMANDER: Good morning, general, I am glad to see you are going to put down the revolt.

NICANDER: Don't you know I am commander-in-chief of the Syrian army?

HYMANDER: Yes. sir; I called you general.

NICANDER: What right have you to call me general? A common piece of truck like you to speak to a man like me. How dare you? Off with you.

AMANDA: This gentleman is my escort.

NICANDER: No matter. He has used words unbecoming a private in the ranks.

HYMANDER: Why, I don't belong to your army.

NICANDER: Then I will see that you do, and as for this maiden, she shall become my servant and wait on me in my tent. *(He takes hold of Amanda.)*

AMANDA: Help! Oh, Hyman, help me!

HYMANDER *(Taking hold of Nicander.)*: You leave that young lady alone!

NICANDER: How dare you speak to me, a Syrian commander-in-chief? *(He takes hold of Amanda.)*

AMANDA: Help! Help! *(Enter Judah and his army.)* Oh, Judah, please, please rescue me from this horrid brute!

JUDAH *(To Nicander.)*: You are under arrest.

NICANDER: Arrest? Don't you know I am commander-in-chief?

JUDAH: Enough! Take him to the guard house!

(Enter messenger.)

NICANDER: Tell the king I am captured.

(The soldiers lead him off. Messenger flees.)

AMANDA *(To Judah.)*: You are a real hero.

JUDAH: A hero to you? We are enemies.

AMANDA: No longer. I am with you now and against the enemy.

HYMANDER: I want to enlist in your army. I am with you heart and soul.

ALL: Hallelujah!

Curtain.

Act III

Scene—*Same as Act I.*
Time—*A few days later than Act II.*
Curtain—*Sarah, Hannah, Dinah enter.*

SARAH: Praise be the Holy One of Israel, who has raised up brave men to defend us.

HANNAH: Yes, Mattathiah and his brave sons.

DINAH: And have you heard their slogan: Who is like unto Thee among the mighty. O Lord? With this battle cry they are sure to win.

SARAH: May it be the will of God.

(Enter Amanda.)

AMANDA: Peace be unto you, my sisters.

SARAH: How dare you call us sisters, you scoffer?

HANNAH: Apostate to the Greeks!

DINAH: Worshipper of false gods!

AMANDA: You seem to think I am all that is left of Greece in Modin.

SARAH: Begone. You are not worthy to stand before us.

AMANDA: Were I not loyal to my country I would be unworthy to live. But I have had my eyes opened. The oppressor is among us. He would enslave me as well as you. My father's house is princely, but the enemy makes no distinction between rich and poor. We are all enemies of his and so am I. Down with the mad tyrant!

HANNAH: And yesterday you mocked us.

AMANDA: It is you who should have mocked me. Misjudge me not. No daughter of the house of Hiram is guilty of treason. Our country must be united to face the foe.

HANNAH: You speak as one inspired.

AMANDA: I am filled with the spirit of our fathers, who fought against time and chance and finally won.

(Enter Hymander. He is dressed as a soldier of the Maccabees.)

HYMANDER: Who is like unto Thee among the mighty?

AMANDA: Who is like unto thee, O soldier of Israel? How becoming a uniform looks on you. I am proud of you. Aren't you, sisters?

DINAH: Is he one of us?

AMANDA: Are you, Hymander?

HYMANDER: A Jew am I with heart and soul. But you needn't call me Hymander any longer. My old name, Hyman, is good enough for me now.

HANNAH: Now you are one of us and we are proud of you.

AMANDA: And I am no longer Amanda, but Miriam. We are all patriots now. Let's go into the market place and watch Hyman drill. When the boys are in camp we'll send him date pudding.

(They all leave. Enter Nicander and messenger.)

NICANDER: See that no one follows. They put me in the guard house and I escaped.

MESSENGER: You, General, captured?

NICANDER: I didn't tell the guard I was a general. I said I was a blacksmith.

MESSENGER: You, General?

NICANDER: Don't betray me and when I return to Syria I will appoint you chief mechanic in the chariot shop.

MESSENGER: Alas, General, we cannot escape. The enemy has hemmed us in on all sides. We are caught in a trap.

NICANDER: What? A handful of yokels routed a trained army of Syria?

MESSENGER: The entire country from Dan to Beer-sheba is up in arms.

NICANDER: It's the king's fault. I told him to send me a hundred thousand soldiers and he sent a battalion of recruits. Doesn't he know these Jews can fight like lions?

MESSENGER: Alas, General, all is lost.

NICANDER: When I see the king I will give him a piece of my mind.

MESSENGER: Hurry, my Lord, or the enemy will discover us!

NICANDER: Who would ever have, thought that I would have to sneak out of this country like a thief in the night. It's all the king's fault.

MESSENGER: Hurry, my Lord, the village folks will see us.

NICANDER: The king had no right to make war in the first place. He's rightly named, mad man. That's what he is—the mad king. Now. where do we go from here?

MESSENGER: Hack to Syria.

NICANDER: Yes, back to Syria in disgrace. The great general. Nicander. defeated by a band of Jews. *(They leave.)*

(Enter Judah, Mattathiah, soldiers and women. Soldier bearing a Menorah. All sing.)

We will praise, O Lord, Thy grace,
  Fountain of all power;
Thou'rt in storm our sheltering place,
  Our protecting tower.
What if foes assail us?
  Lord, our Rock, will smite their sword,
He will never fail us.

JUDAH: Had not the Lord been on our side we could not have won this great victory.

MATTATHIAH: The Syrians had threatened to make us forsake the law of Moses. But the Lord in His mercy answered us in our distress, and made us, who are few and feeble, triumphant. Our victory is the triumph of justice and righteousness. Freedom is again restored. May in all ages God's help never fail whenever men rise up against us and seek our destruction. Praise be the Redeemer of Israel.

(Enter soldiers with Nicander and Messenger.)

A SOLDIER: Syrian soldiers. We captured them as they ran away.

JUDAH: Behold, the Syrian General. We shall keep him as a hostage.

NICANDER: Alas, that mighty Syria must humble herself before the smallest of nations. I surrender.

JUDAH: Who is like unto Thee among the mighty?

ALL: Who is like Thee among the mighty, O Lord?

JUDAH: Let us rededicate our Temple to the Lord, God!

ENTIRE COMPANY *(Singing.)*: We will praise, etc. *(Form a procession with Judah in the lead; march off as the curtain falls.)*

Curtain.

The Unlighted Menorah:
A Hanukkah Fantasy of the Time
of Felix Medelssohn in One Act

CHARACTERS

ABRAHAM MENDELSSOHN-BARTHOLDY
FELIX, his oldest son
LEAH (Abraham's wife), known as *Felicia*
MOSES MENDELSSOHN, Abraham's father *(seen in his dream)*

TIME—*A November evening in the year 1835, a few days before Abraham's death.*
PLACE—*The library of Abraham Mendelssohn's home, the Gartenhaus, in Berlin.*

Before the curtain rises, one hears the sound of a piano played softly behind the scenes. One of Mendelssohn's compositions written before 1835 should be used. Op.15—his fantasie on the "Last Rose of Summer," one of the fantasies of the Op.16, or one of his earlier "Lieder ohne Wrote" would be appropriate. The music continues during the opening scene between Abraham and Leah.

The library of the Mendelssohn home is comfortable and tastefully arrange; the walls are lined with books. The room is lighted by candles in handsome and fantastic holders.

Abraham Mendelssohn, a man of fifty-nine, blind and frail, sits in a large armchair. At his elbow a table covered with books, several loose sheets of music, etc.; a picture in a silver frame; a vase of flowers; a lighted candle on the other side of the table, where a smaller arm-chair stands. Leah, a handsome woman, a few years his junior, stands before the bookcase in the back wall, apparently in search of a volume.

LEAH: I'm sure I put back the volume of Lessing I was reading to you yesterday, Abraham.

ABRAHAM: Do not trouble to look for it, dear. It is so pleasant just to sit here and listen to Felix playing his own songs.

LEAH *(Still searching.)*: But I know I put Lessing on the third shelf!

ABRAHAM: Ah, Lessing—the defender of the Jew, the friend of Moses Mendelssohn. *(With a whimsical little laugh.)* I used to be proud of being the son of Moses Mendelssohn; now I am honored as the father of my son, Felix Mendelssohn-Bartholdy. *(A moment of painful reverie.)* How proud father would have been of Felix—eh, Felicia?

LEAH: But isn't it due to your planning and foresight that Felix has been appointed Kapellmeister at Leipzig?

ABRAHAM: I tried to make the way easy for him. Yes, Felicia, it was better that we turned Christian. Felix has never known the hardship of being a Jew, even a Jew with wealth and family and education. When I think of what my poor father suffered—*(Again drifts into reverie.)*

LEAH: Perhaps the book has fallen back behind the others. *(Thrusts her hand behind the other volumes.)* There is something else here. *(She pulls out an old-fashioned Menorah.)* The old Menorah Tante Jette told me your father had in the old house at Hamburg!

ABRAHAM: Let me see it *(Reaches out his hands.)* I mean let me feel it. *(She places it in his hands and sits across from him in the other arm-chair after laying her book upon the table.)* The old Hanukkah Menorah! I remember how father used to say the blessing over the lights— and we would sing—what was that old Hebrew song?—Ah, Mooz T'Zoor. *(Wistfully.)* I should like to hear Felix play it, but he knows no Jewish songs.

LEAH: But I remember it! *(She hums it softly.)*

ABRAHAM *(Feebly beating time.)*: I can almost see the Hanukkah lights again! Ask Felix to play it for me, dear.

LEAH *(Rising and going to the door of the music room.)*: Felix, father wants you.

FELIX *(Entering.)*: Yes, Father. *(He is young, handsomely dressed.)*

(Leah sits near table going over books.)

ABRAHAM: Just now as you were playing, Felix, I wanted to hear an old Jewish song my father used to love. I would like to have you play it for me, for somethings I am hungry to hear those old melodies again.

FELIX: But I don't know anything about Jewish music, father. *(Picking up the Menorah from his father's lap.)* What a beautiful candlestick.

ABRAHAM *(A trifle sadly.)*: You have never seen it lighted, Felix. At my father's house we lighted it each year on Hanukkah, the Jewish Feast of Lights. If my father had lived you might have gone to his house with me at Hanukkah, Felix, and heard him bless the candles. *(To Leah)*: Perhaps if he had lived we might have remained Jews, Felicia.

FELIX *(Still holding the Menorah, sits on edge of table.)*: It seems strange to think of you as a Jew, father. *(Laughing.)* Why, when I have finished my cantata of "St. Paul" it will be played in all the great churches of Europe. I can't imagine myself writing Jewish music, can you father?

ABRAHAM *(Heavily.)*: No, Felix.

LEAH *(Hastily.)*: Father wants you to play an old Hanukkah hymn. *(Rising.)* I'll see whether I can play it myself first—and if I can, you must listen, Felix, and play it afterwards to father, for I know he prefers your music to me.

ABRAHAM *(With laughing protest.)*: Now, Felicia, you know better than that.

LEAH *(Standing behind his chair and smoothing back his hair.)*: And perhaps the music will drive away the foolish dreams that have been troubling you since your illness.

ABRAHAM *(Feeling for her hand and holding it against his cheek.)*: I am not so ill as you would have me, Leah.

LEAH *(A little wistfully.)*: My old Jewish name!

ABRAHAM: The foolish dreams which come to me in my darkness bring back old memories, Felicia.

(She seems about to speak, then with a caress full of tender understanding she leaves him and walks quietly toward the music room. Felix is about to follow her, then pauses irresolutely at the table, where he stands fingering the Menorah.)

FELIX: A Jewish Hanukkah lamp! And I often forget that grandfather was a Jew. *(Picking up the picture.)* Yet I always liked this picture. He did a great deal for your—for *his* people, didn't he, father?

ABRAHAM: He was a prince among Jews and a Jew among princes, *(Bitterly.)* for he was never ashamed of his faith. I wish I might have loved my religion as he did!

FELIX *(Curiously.)*: I never knew you felt like that, father.

ABRAHAM: Perhaps it is because, having grown blind, I am learning to see clearly what I never saw before. It might have been harder for all of us had we remained Jews, and yet—*(Hastily.)* Do not speak of this to mother, Felix, I would not have her unhappy.

FELIX *(Thoughtfully, as he absently fingers the Menorah.)*: If things had been different—if my grandfather had remained poor and unknown—and you and I would have been born in some miserable ghetto—and I would have written chants for the synagogue and songs for the festivals, instead of music like my "St.Paul" for the Christian Church?

LEAH *(At door.)*: I want you to come and listen while I play the Hanukkah hymn, Felix.

FELIX *(Still dreamily.)*: I'm coming. *(He puts the Menorah on the table and walks thoughtfully toward the music room. At the door he turns to his father and adds:)* Had I been reared a Jew it would have made a great difference in my music, father.

(Abraham is left alone, his head bowed on his breast. The candles in the room have burned lower; the light is very dim. From the next room comes the music of "Mooz T'Zoor," which continues during the scene—first played falteringly, as though Leah were trying to remember the old strain, then with more assurance and finally louder and stronger as Felix plays.)

ABRAHAM *(With a great sob of yearning in his voice.)*: He says Judaism would have made a difference in his music. What a difference it would have made in my life!

(As he sits brooding, a man enters. He is middle-aged, wears a skull-cap and talith. As he crosses to the table he sees the Menorah upon it; he picks it up gently, a smile brightening his ugly face.)

MENDELSSOHN: You have the old Menorah? You still light the Hanukkah candles my son?

ABRAHAM *(Stretching out his hands to him.)*: Father!

MENDELSSOHN *(Without approaching him.)*: I am glad. *(The strain of Moos T'Zoor grows stronger.)* And the old Hanukkah hymn! It is good to be a Jew and love the beautiful old customs of our fathers.

ABRAHAM: But it is not always easy to be a Jew, father! *(Ashamed.)* It was not easy for me, so—*(Stops, confused.)*

MENDELSSOHN *(Quietly.)*: It is never easy to be a Jew, my son. For me it meant hunger and poverty and hatred—yes, bitter hatred and injustice, even after the hunger and the poverty had passed away. *(Sits by the table, across from Abraham.)* Yet it is a great joy to be a Jew. I know I was happy through all my miseries, for I loved my people, and I was sure I would be permitted to help carry on the light.

ABRAHAM: Carry on the light?

MENDELSSOHN: Every Jew is a torch-bearer. We are like runners in the old Greek races. *(Picks up lighted candle from table.)* Each runner bears a torch, which he thrusts into the hand of the man who follows him when he drops out of the race. My father gave me the love and learning and a Jewish mind; I hope I passed on these treasures to my children. What will you give your son for his birthright, Abraham? *(Puts down candlestick.)*

ABRAHAM *(Turning away.)*: Oh, father—father—

MENDELSSOHN *(As though misunderstanding the cause of his grief.)*: Is he not a worthy son?

ABRAHAM: Yes—but he is not a Jew—

MENDELSSOHN: I am sorry for the great grief that has come to you, my child. It is hard for you that he will not carry the light down through the ages—that he will never kindle the candles in this old Menorah and say the Hanukkah blessing over them.

ABRAHAM: But it is I would have sinned—I—

MENDELSSOHN: I know how you would shield him, Abraham. So would I have defended your brothers and you against blame; but my children were always faithful and obedient. *(Rising and approaching a little nearer.)* Do you remember our home, your dear mother, who did not laugh at me when I dared to raise my eyes to her beauty, your sisters, your brothers—how all of you gathered about the table that last Hanukkah before—I went away?

ABRAHAM *(Dreamily.)*: Yes father—I sometimes see it now—as I see you—although my eyes are dark—as one sees things in a dream. We are sitting about the table—I am leaning upon mother's knee—and you—you are lightning the first of the Hanukkah candles. Because I am the youngest and have been ill, you let me say the blessing over the first candle. *(Whimsically.)* I wish I might say it now.

MENDELSSOHN *(In loving pity.)*: You may light the candles—and say the blessing, my son. *(Abraham gropes for the lighted candle on the other side of the table.)*

ABRAHAM *(Eagerly.)*: Give me the candle—the lighted candle, father. It is called the "Shammas," isn't it? Give me the candle, father.

MENDELSSOHN *(Placed lighted candle in his hand.)*: I have given you the lighted candle, my child.

ABRAHAM: Yes *(Joyfully.)* I feel the heat of the flame upon my eyelids. *(Groping with his free hand.)* But I want the Menorah. *(He touches the Menorah and draws it to him.)* Now I will light it. *(As his hand wanders over the Menorah a look of grieved surprise flits across his face.)* Father, I do not think there is any candle here—I cannot find it. *(Faltering.)* Boruch—boruch atto—*(Brokenly.)* I remember the Hebrew of the blessing—but where is the candle?

MENDELSSOHN *(Slowly.)*: My son, I gave you the light, but you have not been able to renew it; you cannot light your Menorah, for your son will never kindle the Hanukkah candles in his own home, nor will his children after him. *(He takes the lighted candles and replaces it across the table. Abraham bows his head over the empty Menorah and sobs like a child.)*

MENDELSSOHN *(His hands lingering for a moment over Abraham's bent head as thought to bless him.)*: But if you remain a good Jew, my son, the light of the Torah will always be a light to give you comfort in your darkness.

ABRAHAM: Father!—I must tell you, oh, father!—*(He gropes to catch Mendelssohn's hand; but Mendelssohn, shaking his head with a strange, wistful smile, passes out into the night. The music in the next room dies away, as Abraham, still half asleep, murmurs brokenly.)* If I could only keep on dreaming—then I could see you father—for I am lonely and cold, and it is dark—

(Felix enters from the music room and hurries to his father.)

FELIX: Father, what is it—are you dreaming again? Father!

ABRAHAM *(Pitifully.)*: The Menorah—I cannot light it—it is empty.

FELIX *(Puzzled.)*: Of course it is empty, father. Why should you want to light it? *(Sits beside him and speaks enthusiastically.)* Do you know, father, that as I sat listening to mother's play, I had the finest inspiration for a new motif in my cantata of "St. Paul." *(With a boyish laugh.)* Oh, you'll be so proud of me when you hear it! Why, by next Christmas it will be played in all the churches in Europe! *(He breaks off to look curiously at his father, who sits with his head bowed over the Menorah, sobbing like a child.)*

ABRAHAM: And the Menorah—will never—be lighted!

By the Light of Hanukkah:
A Play in Three Acts

CHARACTERS

ESTHER, a girl of thirteen, blind. Her eyelids are closed throughout the play.

DAVID, her brother, aged sixteen. A younger boy may play this role, but he must have some ability and experience in amateur dramatics.

BENJAMIN, a younger brother, aged twelve. One with a sense of humor preferred.

THE MOTHER, a girl who can dress up to look the part and who can assume the quiet dignity of a mother

SAMUEL, a cousin of the children, a boy twelve years old

HANNAH, Samuel's sister, a girl of eight

MESSENGER BOY, wearing the cap of a telegraph boy

ACT I—*An Afternoon during Hanukkah.*
ACT II—*Friday Noon of the Same Week.*
Act III—*Friday Evening.*

SCENE—*A living room, simply and neatly furnish. There is a table in the center, on which there are a few books and a lamp. There is an entrance to the kitchen on the left, and an entrance on the right, which leads to the hall and to the street. It is necessary that all the lights of the stage be on one switch, so that all may be extinguished at the same time.*

Act I

Mother is seated at the right, knitting. Esther is sitting at the left, strumming on a mandolin, ukulele, or other stringed instrument. She need not be playing a tune, but merely plucks the strings a few times.

ESTHER *(After a few moments have elapsed, putting down the instrument.)*: Mother, is it almost evening?

MOTHER: Why are you so anxious to know, dear? You have asked so many times!

ESTHER: Brother said that when he comes homes tonight he will bright something for me.

MOTHER: Yes, David is always thoughtful of you. I am so glad that he always thinks of his sister.

ESTHER: But tell me, mother. Is it getting dark?

MOTHER: Yes, dear, it will soon be evening. *(Mother lights the lamp.)* Would you care to hear a good story, Esther? I have a new book from the library.

ESTHER: No, I'd rather read one to you. Please bring me my book, mother.

(The mother takes a large book from the table and tenderly hands it to her. A book is raised type, or braille, can generally be borrowed at the local library. If not, any large volume may serve.)

ESTHER *(Receiving the book.)*: You don't mind hearing these old stories over again? You know I never get tired of them. Which story shall I read?

MOTHER: Read the story about the man who made dolls, the first story in the book.

(Esther opens the book and feeling about on the page finally begins; running her finger slowly along the lines she reads.)

ESTHER *(Reading.)*: Once there was a poor carpenter who loved little children, and he always wanted to make them happy. He had to work very hard all day for a living, but every evening he found a little time to play with the children who came into his shop. He told them stories and taught them songs, and he would always make dolls or toys and give them to the poor children. *(Esther stops reading and speaks to her mother.)*

ESTHER: You know, mother? I think that man must have been a Jew.

MOTHER: Why do you think so, Esther?

ESTHER: Oh, just because, mother. Because he was so kind and loving and friendly. And it's just the way our religion teaches us to be. Oh, I remember when I used to go to Sunday School, before that terrible day when my eyes got hurt, mother, how we were taught to think of others and to make others happy.

(David enters on tiptoes, trying to make no sound.)

ESTHER *(Breaking off the conversation with her mother, cries out in a happy voice.)*: Oh, that's David coming in now. You can't fool me. I hear you, Dave.

(David runs up to her and kisses her. He is carrying a rose in his hand.)

DAVID: Yes, it's Dave all right, and I have something for you.

ESTHER: Oh, what is it?

DAVID: Guess.

ESTHER: It's a flower, a rose! I can smell it.

(David hands the flower to her.)

DAVID: Yes, you always know somehow. It's wonderful how you can guess things.

MOTHER: How did you do at the stand today, Dave? Is it paying any better?

DAVID *(Removing his wraps.)*: No, mother, it's still disappointing. It looks as if I can't possibly save enough money to go to the College next year.

MOTHER: Now, don't worry, my brave boy. Be strong and don't give up. Jews somehow manage to overcome difficulties. You know what a struggle the Maccabees had, or Moses, or David, or any of our heroes. If father were only alive he would have spared you this hard work and losing a year that should have been spent in school. But now you must wait and save a little each day, and next year you will start in at the Rabbinical College and become a good rabbi, just as father wanted you to be.

DAVID: Oh, I won't be a quitter, mother; I'll save enough money to go through the first year of College, and then I'll win scholarships every year. And if I can make any money besides, I'm going to send it home to you.

MOTHER: Don't worry about us, David. We shall always get along somehow. If you will be strong and brave and do well at school, that will be enough to make us happy.

DAVID: Yes, as you always say, there's no use worrying. And especially on Hanukkah, when all Jews should learn to be brave. It's the third light tonight, isn't it?

MOTHER: Yes, the third light. Don't you remember that we lit two last night?

(All the lights on the stage out out.)

DAVID: What the matter with the electric light, anyhow?

MOTHER: I don't know. *(Lights go on.)* That has happened twice this week. Last time they were out ten minutes along the street.

DAVID: Oh, yes, but wasn't it nice watching the Hanukkah candles burning in the dark? It reminded me of the verse in the Bible, how when the plague of darkness came in Egypt all the children of Israel had light in their dwellings. I don't mind if electricity does go off for a while if we have Hanukkah candles burning.

MOTHER: Well, I must leave you a while.

ESTHER: Mother, are you going?

MOTHER: Yes, child, I must set the dishes on the table.

ESTHER: Oh, let me help you. I'll arrange the knives and forks.

(Esther feels her way about and with a little assistance from David passes out through the kitchen entrance.)

DAVID *(Calling.)*: Mother!

MOTHER *(Having just stepped out, looks in from the kitchen entrance.)*: Yes?

DAVID: I'm going to practice my part for the Hanukkah play. You won't mind it I make a little noise will you?

MOTHER: No, go right ahead.

(David takes a paper from his pocket and lays it on the table, steps to one side, strikes a pose, and begins to recite dramatically.)

DAVID: Begone, ye Syrians, away! My trusty sword shall drive you out. *(He makes a gesture as though flourishing a sword.)* Oh, they flee! And you, Haman, I tell thee, on my word. *(Pauses.)* No, that can't be right. What's Haman got to do with Hanukkah? Why, I'm getting my lines from the last Purim play mixed up in this. *(Looks at paper and memorizes, then begins again.)* Begone, ye Syrians, away! My trusty sword shall drive you out! *(Repeats the gesture.)* An ere another day has passed our people shall be free.

(Benjamin entering throws his cap on a chair and applauds.)

BENJAMIN: Good boy! Hurrah for our Judah Maccabee. Do you know? You're a pretty good actor, little brother.

DAVID *(Making a rush at him seizes him by the throat.)*: And you, Apollonius, the leader of this Syrian horde—

BENJAMIN: Hands off, I'm not a Syrian. I'm a Jew.

DAVID *(Releasing him.)*: It's lucky for you you spoke just then. You know, we actors are very temperamental.

BENJAMIN *(Taking off his coat.)*: I don't know what that big word means; but I guess it's something like craziness.

DAVID: Oh, you don't understanding anything. But don't interfere with the play. Take a seat and I shall enlighten you.

BENJAMIN *(Seating himself.)*: Say, Dave, I heard something today and I'm wondering it it's true.

DAVID: What's that?

BENJAMIN: Cousin Sam told me that a big doctor said our Esther's eyes are perfectly all right, only that when our house caught on fire two years ago and she was alone in the burning room until the fireman saved her, she was so frightened that she lost her sight. But her eyes weren't hurt. It was just the scare that made her blind.

DAVID: Yes, we know all that.

BENJAMIN: But Sam told me that the big doctor said that if she went through something very exciting again she might get her sight back.

DAVID: Sure, I heard that long ago.

BENJAMIN: Then why don't we give her a scare, so that poor Esther will be able to see again?

DAVID: Well, because there's more to the story. Another shock might not work that way. You never can tell. Too much excitement might drive her insane or even kill her. Now do *you* think you'd like to scare her?

BENJAMIN: I'll say I don't. I guess I didn't understand it all before.

(Mother enters.)

MOTHER: Come, boys, it's time for supper.

DAVID: Oh, dear, when will I learn those last few lines of my Hanukkah part? Just four more days till the performance. I'm afraid I'll make a failure of it and spoil the whole thing. And I'm so anxious to make it a success.

BENJAMIN: How about the Hanukkah lights tonight, mother?

MOTHER: I have them on the kitchen table.

BENJAMIN: All right. I'm ready for the service and the supper, too. Come on, David, this will help your—your—you know, that funny thing you've got. I mean your temperament.

Curtain.

ACT II

Lunch is set on the table in the same room. Kitchen chairs are drawn up to the table. Esther is seated at the left polishing a few pieces of silverware. She is humming the Hanukkah hymn, "Rock of Ages." She is alone for a few moments. Mother enters. She carries an unopened letter.

MOTHER: You have worked long enough on those knives and forks, Esther. They are bright and shining now. *(Takes them from her and carries them to the table.)*

ESTHER: Are they really, mother? It makes me so happy to think that I can make things look nice and pleasing for others, even though I cannot see them.

MOTHER: It shall not always be this way, Esther. Surely you shall not always dwell in darkness. I feel certain that some day you will be able to see again the loveliness that you create. *(Puts her arm around her.)*

ESTHER: Oh, I see lots of things now, mother. I see the kindness and love around me. And I can always see when there is a smile on your face, for I heard the smile in your voice.

MOTHER: Am I smiling now, Esther?

ESTHER: No, you are troubled and anxious about something. What is it, mother?

MOTHER: It may be something very good. I do not know. It may be a great blessing, or it may be a message that will make us unhappy. It is a letter that came today from the American Rabbinical College for David. I am wondering what is in it. I am waiting for him to come home, for I never open his mail.

ESTHER: A letter from the College? For David! Oh, I wonder what it says! Maybe they want him to come right away. Maybe some good man has offered to pay his expenses. Then all his worry would be over. Oh, I wish that David would hurry. He ought to be home soon. I hear someone on the stairs. Maybe he is coming now.

(Enter Benjamin, Samuel and Hannah.)

BENJAMIN: Hello, everybody. My! Its great outside, a little bit cold, but it's so bright and clear that I'm going to take Esther out for a walk after school. *(Looks around.)* Are we going to eat in here today?

MOTHER: Yes, we are fixing up the kitchen for Shabbos. And it's nice to change things around occasionally. David says he gets tired of eating in the kitchen all the time.

BENJAMIN *(Removing his wraps.)*: It's a nice kitchen. Who says it isn't? And when I get rich I'm going to buy us a big house, with a dining room, and a library, and a sun-parlor, and a great big garden, and three kitchens.

ESTHER: And don't forget the piano you promised me.

BENJAMIN: Oh, I'm not forgetting. Only I haven't got the money just yet. But look who's here! Cousin Sam and Cousin Hannah. Gee, ain't they the bashful kids! They haven't said a word since they came in.

MOTHER: You haven't given them a chance. How are you, children?

SAMUEL: Very well, thank you, Aunt Libby.

HANNAH *(Courtesies.)*: Yes, we're very well, thank you, Aunt Libby.

MOTHER: Won't you take off your coats and have lunch with us.

SAMUEL: No, thanks, we're on our way home. Mother is expecting us.

MOTHER: Then take off your wraps and stay a while. You will have plenty of time for a visit.

SAMUEL: Well, just for a few minutes, Aunt Libby.

HANNAH: Just for a few minutes, Aunt Libby.

(Samuel helps Hannah remove her coat; then takes off his own.)

ESTHER: Oh, Hannah, come and sit on my lap. You always said you were my little girl. *(Hannah goes to Esther.)*

SAMUEL: We just came up to see David and tell him how well he acted his part in the Hanukkah play last night. I thought he would be home already.

ESTHER: David does everything well.

BENJAMIN *(To mother.)*: I see you have a letter for me. Has the President written to me again?

(David enters.)

DAVID: What's this, a surprise party? *(Takes off his coat.)*

MOTHER: Oh, David, I'm so glad you are home. There's a letter for you from the American Rabbinical College.

DAVID *(Taking the letter.)*: This is the first I have received since the one in April, the one I didn't answer.

(Having opened the letter, he reads:)

Mr. David Fleischman,

Dear Sir:

On June 26th I wrote to inform you that your application for admission to the American Rabbinical College had been favorably received and reminding you that, "although tuition at the American Rabbinical College is absolutely free, none the less students entering the College must come prepared to support themselves completely during at least their first year of attendance." You did not reply to this letter, and it was assumed that you had abandoned the intention to enter this institution.

I have just been informed by a student of the College, whose home is in your city, that you are still desirous of becoming a rabbi and that you are working this year to earn the necessary money for your maintenance at the American Rabbinical College next year.

May I suggest that you should have informed the College of this fact? On rare occasions scholarships have been given to boys who are entering the College. One scholarship was available this year for an entering student, which might have been granted to you because of the high honors you achieved in your High School work and the splendid recommendations which accompanied your application.

Regretting that there has been a misunderstanding, and with all good wishes, I am

Very sincerely yours,
Dr. Eli Seligman, Registrar.

(David stares at the letter as though dazed.)

MOTHER: What a pity! Had you written them and told them your difficulty, they might have helped you out. Now I'm afraid they are angry with you for not writing.

DAVID: But I thought it would be useless. Just think! If I had only known this!

BENJAMIN: Tough luck, David. I don't quite understand it. But it looks as if you lost something.

DAVID: Lost something? Yes, a year of my life, I could have been at College instead of selling magazines at a railway station.

SAMUEL: Do you mind explaining it, David? I don't quite understand.

DAVID: It's simple enough. Dr. Seligman wrote my last spring that they do not accept students at the American Rabbinical College unless they can afford to pay their own way through the first year. Then, if they make good and their folks can't support them, their way is paid until they graduate. That is, they can get high marks and win scholarships. Well, I didn't answer that letter because I had no money to pay my way through the first year, and I thought I'd wait and make a new application next year. But now Dr. Seligman writes that they would have made an exception in my case and helped me pay my way this year. Oh, what a fool I've been!

ESTHER: It's not your fault, David.

DAVID: Not my fault? Of course it's my fault.

MOTHER: It may not be too late yet.

DAVID: Yes, it's too late this year. It's more than two months since the school session began.

MOTHER: But, David, you've been studing right along just what you've been missing at the College. Every evening you have been doing your work so that it would be easier for you next year. You could catch up with the others quickly. Write to Dr. Seligman. It may not be too late.

BENJAMIN: Sure, write to them, David.

MOTHER: By all means; sit down and prepare a letter at once.

ESTHER: Please do, David, sit down and write a letter to the College.

DAVID *(His sense of humor getting the better of him.)*: Well, Hannah, what do you advise?

HANNAH: I always do what my mother tells me.

DAVID: And so will I. But supposing I send a telegram, mother. I might get an answer today. Oh, wouldn't it be wonderful if I could get that scholarship!

MOTHER: You will find paper and pen in the kitchen. Go in and prepare a telegram.

(David leaves.)

SAMUEL: We'll have to be going. We've stayed longer than we should.

MOTHER: You are still welcome to lunch with us.

HANNAH: Thank you, Aunt Libby; we'll come some other time.

BENJAMIN: You forgot to congratulate David on his acting in the Hanukkah play last night. Wait a few minutes and you can tell him how well he did. It will make him feel better.

SAMUEL: Oh, we'll see him some other time. He's too busy now to talk about the play. *(They start to leave.)*

BENJAMIN: Don't go yet. I got an idea. You can leave the telegram at the telegraph office down the street on your way home. It won't take you a minute and it will save time for David.

DAVID *(Coming out of the kitchen.)*: How's this, mother?

"Dr. Eli Seligman,
Chicago, Illinois:
    Have kept up in all studies. Would enter college now if scholarship were granted.

David Fleischman."

That's fourteen words; but it's the best I can do.

MOTHER: That seems very good. Samuel will send it off for you.

DAVID: I think I'd rather send it myself and be sure that it's sent.

MOTHER: You know that Samuel is thoroughly reliable.

DAVID: Yes, that's so. He's a true boy scout. Here it is, Sam. And here's a dollar. You can give me the change any time.

SAMUEL *(Taking the telegram and money.)*: I'll send it right away. Goodbye, everybody.

ALL: Goodbye.

MOTHER: Come, again, often.

(Hannah and Samuel leave.)

DAVID: Just think, if I had written to Dr. Seligman last May, as I should have—

BENJAMIN *(Seated at the table, unfolding his napkin.)*: Then you'd have missed this good meal.

DAVID: Oh, you joke about everything.

BENJAMIN: Do you want me to cry?

DAVID: Well, don't you care about the fact that I may be able to go to Chicago soon, maybe tomorrow night? And maybe I'll have to wait a year. And maybe I'll never be able to save enough money and never get a chance to study.

BENJAMIN: Of course I care. Didn't I offer to work all next summer and give you everything I can earn, so that you'd have plenty of money to go to College?

ESTHER: But maybe now, Bennie, you will be able to keep the money you will earn for yourself.

BENJAMIN: Oh, no, I won't keep it. If David doesn't need it, I'm going to buy the house with it. Do you think we'll be able to get a nice house for fifty dollars?

MOTHER: Don't be silly, Benjamin. Come, David, sit down to lunch.

DAVID: I can't eat any lunch now. My appetite is spoiled. I'm too excited to eat now.

MOTHER: That will never do. No matter what happens, you must never let yourself be upset. Even though this may be the most important day of our lives, we must be self-possessed.

(They take their places at the table.)

MOTHER: David, will you say a prayer?

(All bow their heads.)

DAVID: Heavenly Father, for all Thy good gifts we praise and thank Thee. May Thy love watch over us and sustain us. And may the spirit of the Maccabees inspire us. Amen.

(They break bread. Pause.)

DAVID: Mother, I just can't stop thinking. What answer will the College send me?

BENJAMIN: Open up the covered dish. I think the answer I'm looking for is in there.

Curtain.

ACT III

Esther, David, and Benjamin are seated in the same room. It is Friday evening and the mother is lighting the Shabbos candles, which are placed at the ends of the table. Between these two candles is a Hanukkah Lamp with eight candles and Shamos in place. The mother, standing behind the table, lights the Shabbos candles and speaks.

MOTHER: May the beams of the Sabbath light gladden our hearts, O Lord. At this hour turn Thou the hearts of the parents to the children and the hearts of the children to the parents, and may Thy love abide with all of us. Bless Thou our children, O our Father. Help them to walk in Thy truth and enable them to become a blessing unto Israel and unto all mankind. May every Sabbath bring new blessings. Amen.

(Pause.)

DAVID: Mother, it doesn't seem like Shabbos.

MOTHER: Why not?

DAVID: On Sabbaths it is always so peaceful and lovely here. Tonight it isn't so!

MOTHER: Why, David! How you surprise me! It is calm and peaceful here.

DAVID: No. I feel that I could scream out in pain. I can't sit still. The whole world seems to be spinning around.

MOTHER: You are excited David, and no wonder. You feel that your life hangs in the balance. But it is why the Sabbath is given to us, that we may rest and be assured that God will make all things right if we are worthy of His kindness. Even if your telegram should not be answered, or even if your request is refused, some day in some other way you will accomplish your aim in life.

BENJAMIN: Funny how a fellow can be so two-sided. He played Judah Maccabeus last night like a real hero. You'd have thought he was the bravest man in creation. He stood up there like a sure enough soldier and said—What was it?—Oh, yes, "We children of Israel can laugh to scorn our enemies; nothing can injure us when we serve the Lord." And now look at him—he's all broken up already.

DAVID: No, I'm not broken up. But you'd be pretty much worried too if your whole life depended on a telegram.

ESTHER: But it isn't your whole life. As mother says, even if they won't give you a scholarship now, you will win out in the end. Hasn't mother always taught us not to be afraid of the harder and longer road?

BENJAMIN: There's no use arguing with him any more. What he needs is some of that Maccabean spirit. Let's light the Hanukkah candles. They ought to have been lit before the Shabbos candles, anyhow. But let's get them lit now. And when my little brother David sees the Hanukkah lights it might remind him that he belongs to a brave people and that ought to brace up a bit.

DAVID: Very well. You're right at that. If I want to be a rabbi and deal with big, important things of the whole Jewish people, I oughtn't to be so upset by my own little affairs. Come, Esther, you're to say the blessings. And Ben will light four candles and I'll light four.

(David and Ben lead Esther to her place. The three stand behind the table, one of the boys on each side of Esther. While she is speaking, David lights the Shamos and with it four of the candles. He passes the Shamos to Benjamin, who lights the other four.)

ESTHER: *Boruch atoh adonoy, elohenu melech haolom, asher kidshonu b'mitsvosov v'tsivonu l'hadlik ner shel Hanukkah.*
Blessed art Thou, O Lord our God, King of the Universe, who hast sanctified us by Thy commandments and hast commanded us to kindle the light of Hanukkah.
Boruch atoh adonoy, elohenu melech haolom, sheosah nisim laavosenu bayomim hohem bazman hazeh.

Blessed art Thou, O Lord our God, King of the Universe, who wrought miracles for our fathers in the days of old, at this season.

BENJAMIN: Well said. Now if we can have supper, mother, we shall still be on time for Temple.

MOTHER: I'm sorry that the supper is late. But we shall have to wait now until the potatoes boil. I'm afraid I have been thinking too much of David's telegram this afternoon.

BENJAMIN *(Running to the door.)*: I hear the telegraph boy. *(He runs out.)*

DAVID *(Running after him excitedly.)*: Has he come?

BENJAMIN *(Returning.)*: No, I just wanted to see if you'd keep cool. How you disappoint me!

ESTHER: Bennie, if you don't stop tormenting David—

BENJAMIN: I've got it! I know exactly what's happened. Everything's all right. You don't have to wait for an answer. No use worrying. Come on, brace up, David. It's all fixed Sammy must have forgotten to send your telegram.

ESTHER: Oh, Bennie. Can't you ever stop teasing? You're a little nuisance.

BENJAMIN: Yes, but think what a sad place this old world would be without me!

MOTHER: I don't think we'll be any the sadder if you will keep quiet for the next few minutes. Esther can tell us the story of Hanukkah. It's more interesting than your pranks.

ESTHER: Oh, yes, let me tell you about Hanukkah. But the boys must sit at my feet while I tell it, like we used to sit at your feet, mother, when we were little.

BENJAMIN: I used to sit on mother's lap.

ESTHER: But you're a big boy now. Or do you think you're still a baby?

BENJAMIN: All right. The floor's good enough for me.

(The boys are seated. Esther puts her hands on their heads to see that they are there; then sits back and begins.)

ESTHER: It was in the year 165 B.C.E. That was long before America was discovered and before there were any Christians, but the Jews had already been a people for two thousand years. And they had returned from their exile in Babylonia and were living peacefully in Palestine. But they were under Syrian rule. You see, the Syrian kings made them pay taxes, but they didn't bother them much, until there came one Syrian king, Antiochus Epiphanes, who was very greedy and very cruel. He wanted to make all of them worship idols, so that they would be like his other subjects.

DAVID: Yes, tyrants want all the people to be exactly alike, so that they can handle them more easily. But in a democracy like the United states everyone is permitted to follow his own religion. That's what our teacher told us in school.

ESTHER: But Antiochus was a tyrant. And he sent his soldiers into Palestine to set up idols. They ordered the Jews to worship these idols. In the town of Modin there was an old priest whose name was Matathias. He threw down the idol and drove off the soldier and started a revolution. He had five sons, the bravest of whom was Judah—Judah the Maccabee. And under his leadership the Jews fought many battles and drove out the Syrian armies. The Syrians had set up idols in the Temple and defiled the Sanctuary. But the Maccabees recaptured it and purified it and restored the worship of the one true God. There's a whole lot more to the story, of course but that's the important part.

BENJAMIN: I should say there's a lot more. You didn't even mention Hannah and her seven sons, nor the oil that lasted seven days, nor how Eliezer was killed by an elephant, and lots of other things.

MOTHER: I think supper is ready now. Come, Esther, we shall set the food on the table. And the Sabbath lights, too.

(The mother goes to take the candles, but each of the boys say, "I'll carry them." Each boy takes one of the Sabbath candles and carries it into the kitchen. Esther and the mother follow the out.)

(The boys quickly return to the living room. Bennie is speaking as they enter.)

BENJAMIN: But, David, I thought you said you weren't going to the Temple tonight. You said you were going to wait here and see if an answer would come to your telegram this evening.

DAVID: Well, I feel differently about it now. Perhaps the answer from the College will be sent by letter and won't get here till Monday. Anyhow, I'm going to be less excited. *(Lowers his voice.)* You know how dangerous too much excitement may be for Esther.

BENJAMIN: That's right. Let's be careful.

DAVID: To tell the truth, Bennie, I'm praying with all my heart and soul that they'll give me the scholarship. I can't possibly earn enough during the next year to keep me the following year at College. The stand isn't paying well at all. You know I took the job on commission. It seemed to be a paying proposition. But I'm not making much at all. I've have to get another position, and good jobs are very scarce. I don't want to tell mother; I don't want to worry her.

BENJAMIN: That's too bad, brother. But you know somehow I feel that it will come out all right. There's something wonderful abut mother. The way she always has hope and faith. It's inspiring. I'm just a happy go lucky kid, but I realize how much mother has gone through, and how she always comes out smiling and trusting in God. Just think how different our home would be if mother were discouraged and complaining. It's easy to be brave with such a mother.

DAVID: Right you are, Bennie. I never knew you had so much sense.

(Knocking is heard from without.)

DAVID: There is someone at the door.

(He hurries out. Benjamin goes to the same door, the one leading to the hallway and street, and stands there looking out a moment. Then he hurries to the kitchen, calling out, "The messenger boy's here." David enters with the messenger boy.)

MESSENGER BOY *(Holding open his delivery book.)*: A telegram for David Fleischman.

DAVID: Well I'm David Fleischman.

(Bennie, followed by Esther and Mother, enters from the kitchen.)

MESSENGER BOY: What time is it?

DAVID *(Looks at watch or clock.)*: Seven o' clock.

(Messenger writes the time of delivery into his book, hands David the telegram and leaves.)

DAVID: Here it is, the answer.

MOTHER: Let's hear it.

BENJAMIN: I can hardly wait.

(David tears open the envelope and is drawing out the message, when all the stage lights are extinguished.)

DAVID: Now, what do you think of that?

ESTHER: What's the matter? What does it say? Why doesn't David read the telegram to us?

MOTHER: The lights went out and David can't see to read it. But, David, you *can* read it. Come over here to the candles. You can read it by the Hanukkah lights.

(David reaches over toward the light, straightens the telegram and reads.)

DAVID: Come at once. Scholarship granted.

(David shouts for joy. Benjamin, too, yells, "Wow! Hurrah! Isn't that great!")

MOTHER: How wonderful! Oh, David, how fortunate we are! Esther, did you hear? David is to go to college right away.

ESTHER *(Who has opened her eyes just as the mother speaks her name.)*: Yes mother. Oh, mother, mother. I see! I can see! I see the lights of Hanukkah!

(Esther speaks this very slowly, pausing between each of the phrases.)

Curtain.

Note About the Book

This collection features the work of Jacob J. Leibson, an author of religious children's stories and plays; Ruth E. Levi; the Rabbis: Rev. Dr. Alexander Lyons, Solomon Fineberg, Joseph Leiser, and Louis Witt; Imra Kraft, an author of educational children's plays; the vice president of the Union of American Hebrew Congregations, Louis Broido and Elma Levinger, a teacher and activist who dedicated her writing career to producing work that would instill a sense of pride in Jewish children.

A Note from the Publisher

Spanning many genres, from non-fiction essays to literature classics to children's books and lyric poetry, Mint Edition books showcase the master works of our time in a modern new package. The text is freshly typeset, is clean and easy to read, and features a new note about the author in each volume. Many books also include exclusive new introductory material. Every book boasts a striking new cover, which makes it as appropriate for collecting as it is for gift giving. Mint Edition books are only printed when a reader orders them, so natural resources are not wasted. We're proud that our books are never manufactured in excess and exist only in the exact quantity they need to be read and enjoyed. To learn more and view our library, go to minteditionbooks.com

bookfinity & MINT EDITIONS

Enjoy more of your favorite classics with Bookfinity,
a new search and discovery experience for readers.
With Bookfinity, you can discover more vintage
literature for your collection, find your Reader Type,
track books you've read or want to read,
and add reviews to your favorite books.
Visit www.bookfinity.com, and click on
Take the Quiz to get started.

Don't forget to follow us
@bookfinityofficial and @mint_editions

The Big Festival of Lights

Stories and Plays for Hanukkah